DONT TREAD ON ME

A Boy Sailor *with* JOHN PAUL JONES

By
H. C. THOMAS

Illustrated by
HENRY E. VALLELY

WHITMAN PUBLISHING COMPANY
RACINE, WISCONSIN

TABLE OF CONTENTS

Noah, Hat in Hand, Approached His Master

A BOY SAILOR

With John Paul Jones

CHAPTER ONE

THE BOUND-BOY AND HIS MASTER

Lady, the ailing, underfed mare, dragged the crude oak-and-iron plow to the end of the furrow near the split-rail fence and halted. Twisting her neck, she bit fretfully at the ragged harness that with every step chafed more painfully the raw sores of her shoulders.

Noah Carr—at sixteen sinewy and tall as a grown man—hesitated at the plow handles, frowning. His glance found a good third of the Virginia tobacco field still to be turned over in black ribbons. And Angus MacAuliffe, his master, would require that it be finished before sundown.

Yet watching the mare strive to nuzzle the be-patched harness from her sores, Noah felt pity well up in him, and resentment. For he hadn't so much as a rag pad or replacement strap to ease the faithful horse's pain. Angus MacAuliffe was not one to spend a King's shilling to ease the lot of any man or beast he owned while the creature had strength to earn him another farthing. Noah had learned that fact again last eventide as, hat in hand, he approached his master slouched in a chair on the veranda of his mansion.

"Sir, could we not have Negro Will fashion the mare a new harness? The plowing would get done the quicker for't. And I fear Lady won't be working long, else, but dying."

"New harness?" the red-faced, gouty MacAuliffe snarled. "First ye want the nag retired because she's sick. Now 'tis a new harness ye ask for that bag o' bones! No! She's already eaten twice her worth, and must work for't. Do ye expect a colonial plow-horse turned out like His Majesty's coach-and-six in London?"

He slouched lower in his chair. With fingers that shook from the liquor that was always in him, Angus MacAuliffe pinched snuff from an ornate gold box and sniffed it into nostrils that were like nail-holes in a spout. He gestured dismissal.

"Plow, and hold your peace. But if ye forget again that you're but a bound-boy, there'll be the lash to remind ye!"

Watching the horse's suffering, Noah angrily hurled his reins to the ground. He strode to Lady's shoulder and opened the buckles of her harness. Then he forked his long legs over the fence, returning in a moment with cool leaves from plants in the forest which had been thrust back to give Angus MacAuliffe a field.

"These'll help a tiny bit, Lady," he soothed, and gently laid them on the raw flesh of her shoulder. "Master or no master, we'll be resting awhile."

Shooing the flies away, Noah stood stroking the mare's neck until the sound of hoofbeats along the rutty highway to Fredericksburg made him turn. There was sharp apprehension lest Angus MacAuliffe discover him not laboring under the hot sun. But it changed to relief as he saw that neither of the two oncoming riders was his master.

The smaller, green-habited rider waved before they were within earshot. Noah, snatching off his hat, waved it in return. He could not tell who the man rider was, but Eileen always was welcome. She was cheery and kind and true-hearted, though 'twas scarce understandable since she had the same blood and name as Noah's master. From Edenton, in North Carolina, came Eileen, fifteen-year-old niece of Angus MacAuliffe. And her presence contributed one note, at least, of happiness to this plantation—though Noah hated to think how dreary 'twould be when Eileen returned home.

As the riders slowed their mounts, he walked across the plowed furrows to the fence bordering the highway. The man with Eileen, he saw, was short and had wide, powerful shoulders. He sat his horse well enough, though lacking the ease of the typical Virginian. But he looked a gentleman, from his somewhat haughty manner and his well-made Williamsburg coat with its satin lapels and the lace at his throat and the kerchief tucked into the cuff of one sleeve.

Eileen, wearing a saucy, feathered hat and dark green jacket and skirt, relaxed in her side-saddle position as Noah grasped her bay's headstall strap.

"How goes the plowing, Noah?" She smiled, gazing over the field. "You've fair slathered up the black earth in a lovely design. Like a striped dress for Mother Nature."

"It goes well enough, Miss Eileen. Have you had a fine ride?"

"Oh, yes. Captain," she addressed the stranger, who was doubtless twice her age, "may I present Noah Carr? He—er—is with my Uncle Angus. Noah, meet Captain John Paul Jones. He has sailed the seven seas and, I doubt not, covered himself with glory, if 'twere but visible. Though I am but a child, Noah—as dear Papa likes to remind me—have I not made a pretty catch?" she ended archly.

"Madame," Captain Jones assured her, "you have captured this old merchantman, and I doubt not will sink me ere ten minutes more!"

Eileen's oval face was the prettier in laughter and

her dark curls danced like the lights of her brown eyes. It made Noah Carr chuckle, the gay sauciness of her. Eileen was so much fun always—even, betimes, beguiling the sour Angus MacAuliffe into something less than his usual scowl.

Captain Jones's oddly faded blue eyes made a thorough study of Noah.

"At your command, Captain," Noah said respectfully.

"Your servant, Noah." He gazed at the mare a distance away. "I am but a seafaring man and know little of horses, but is not that poor beast too ill to plow? Look at her sores!"

Noah nodded. " 'Twould be far better if we did not work her." He dared say no more lest he criticize his master.

" 'T seems to me she's half-dead. As if she can't do five more furrows the field's length without dropping."

"Yes, sir." Noah kicked a tuft of grass. " 'Twill be a mercy when she finds the freedom of death, poor Lady."

"La! Freedom again," sighed Eileen MacAuliffe. "Tell me, Captain Jones, why does everyone keep talking freedom? Noah forever discusses it, and similarly our elders. But see, I have freedom to ride—with only Zel attending me." She indicated the mounted Negro groom waiting ten yards behind her. "Since my schooling, I have freedom to wait my coming-out when I'm sixteen, and then to marry if I want. With Papa's consent, of course," she added. "But—"

"You do not have real freedom. None of us has, Miss Eileen," Noah told her. "I, for example—"

"Oh, you will have it when you're twenty-one. Do not fret about it, Noah," Eileen urged kindly. To Captain Jones she explained, "Noah is indentured to Uncle Angus. And it chafes him like the harness chafes poor Lady yonder. He cannot understand why his mother indentured him. Noah expected to grow up a gentleman, but his mother died and there he was, a bound-boy. Oh!" Eileen clapped a small hand over her mouth. "Noah, I am sorry. La, I do rant on about your personal affairs. Forgive me, dear Noah."

He could not help a little smile because she was so conscience-stricken. "It is unimportant, except we mustn't burden the Captain."

He felt the faded blue eyes studying him. "Sometimes," Captain Jones comforted, "character grows stronger in misfortune. Your father, Noah?"

He felt himself reddening. "I don't recall him, sir. We lived in Trinidad and I was but five when he died. We stayed on there until Mother sold everything, as the climate was ill for her. Later, in Norfolk, she took typhoid and died on my fourteenth birthday."

"Ah." Captain Jones swung from his saddle and busied himself at its cinch. Leaning against his horse, he said, "The sort of freedom much discussed these days, Miss Eileen, is the political sort. It concerns His Majesty, King George the Third, laying onerous taxes on the colonies. And not giving us representation in Parliament. I fear His Majesty has heeded bad advice."

"And as a result may one day find rebellion on his hands," Noah declared. "For people will not long abide tyranny!"

The pale eyes twinkled. "A firebrand, eh?"

"Well," Eileen said and pouted, "I don't care so much about liberty, but Papa says also the King does treat our colonies badly. Papa says the Tea Tax is an outrage. He says some men of Boston became so furious about it that they dressed like Indians and stole aboard a vessel and flung its whole cargo of tea into the harbor! And Papa says maybe he'll join the Sons of Liberty if the Stamp Act isn't repealed, and the quartering of soldiers in people's homes isn't stopped. And now Papa has traveled all the way to Philadelphia to discuss with men who think as he does, and—"

She stopped for lack of breath, her cheeks flushed at the smiles of Captain Jones and Noah.

Eileen slid from her saddle. "If I were a man, I'd

not bide oppression! I'd fight, if need be, like my Papa intends to!"

"Madame, our smiles were born of your fervor, not of your words," explained Captain Jones. "And many believe as you do."

"Dr. Franklin of Philadelphia says—" Noah began.

"You know of Dr. Franklin?"

"I like his 'Poor Richard's Almanac' very much," Noah declared. "He prints in that book good advice like, 'Early to bed and early to rise makes a man healthy, wealthy, and wise.' Although much sleep has not seemed to gain me either wealth or wisdom," he added ruefully.

Captain Jones laughed. Sobering, he regarded Eileen and Noah as a parent might.

"Permit me," he said, "a word of counsel to you rather hotheaded young people. There is much talk of rebellion against King George. But do you think the King, who is our ruler, will permit rebellion?"

"But, sir, when a king is tyrannous and unjust and—"

"Our views are doubtless much alike, Noah," Captain Jones conceded. "But as master of a ship, I never permitted rebellion. I crushed it a-borning and dealt out severe punishment. And is not the King master of a ship, in a way of thinking?

"Take the advice of one older than yourselves,"

he urged, laying a friendly hand on Noah's shoulder. "We agree that the King has heeded bad advice, and that the colonies seethe with resentment. But remember, the King has his partisans, and plenty of them, here in Virginia and elsewhere. So one should not trust baring his views to anyone within earshot. There are spies everywhere. We, who believe the colonies should have their rights, may never see them got if we're hanged for not observing caution."

There was a pause.

Eileen tossed her head. "La," she said contemptuously, "no one shall hang me. Shouldn't I look a fool, dangling in the breeze!"

The others burst out laughing, and Eileen, with a roguish glint in her eyes, showed she had said it to turn from seriousness to gaiety.

Captain Jones was whacking his thigh when Noah's laughter died and hot startlement went through him. He stiffened, his gaze on the man tipped forward as he bestrode a horse whose trudging approach on the rutty highway had gone unheard in their talk.

Eileen saw, and caught her breath. Captain Jones, following their looks, shot the girl and Noah a keen glance.

The horse veered off the road toward them and at a vicious jerk of the reins, halted. Angus Mac-

Auliffe sat sullen and silent, his shoulders bowed forward, his face redder than usual and blotchy, his head somewhat lowered so that he had to peer upward at them from the shade of his hat tipped slouchily forward. He looked much the worse for prolonged drinking at The Red Bull tavern a few miles distant at Wadleigh's Corners. He had gone there last evening after Noah asked for new harness for the mare; nor had he returned all night nor this morning, and it was now past mid-afternoon.

"Your servant, Mr. MacAuliffe," Captain Jones said agreeably.

The bloodshot eyes wrenched from Noah Carr to regard him.

"Yuservat," he mumbled. "Cap'ain Paul."

"Jones, if you please, sir."

The sullen eyes pinned him. "Cap'ain Paul," he said again, deliberately. "John Paul. 'S your name. Isn't it?"

"My name," the Captain stated with an edge to his tone, "is John Paul Jones, at your service."

"Changed 't, maybe. How long since?"

Noah saw the Captain's rather sharp face lose color and his eyes take on a steely glint. "Mr. MacAuliffe, as your well-meaning neighbor, sir, let me suggest that you refrain from testing any man's honor until your—er—health is improved."

The planter kept staring offensively. "Honor?

Did ye say honor?" As if aware that he was close to open insult, he kept watching Captain Jones. "Too many spies about," Angus MacAuliffe grumbled. "Talk of freedom 'n' rebellion by a lot of loose-mouths."

There was silence. Noah, standing taut, saw Captain Jones immobile as a statue. His eyes blazed, and plainly only with a great effort could he control himself.

"La, Uncle," Eileen put in with a forced laugh, "shall we ride to the house? This is serious talk for such a sunny day!"

Her effort failed and she sat miserably silent. Captain Jones had not moved a muscle. Fire blazed in his eyes in a way that made Noah thankful it was not directed at him. When the Captain spoke his words rang like metal.

"There is also, Mr. MacAuliffe, too much tippling —all night tippling," he said pointedly. "The loose-mouths you refer to oft are made looser by liquor."

He turned. "My respects to you, Noah. Madame, I am much in your debt for refreshing companionship on our brief ride." He swung on his horse, obviously wanting to depart before compelled to come to blows with Angus MacAuliffe. "Good day, all," he said, and putting his mount to a brisk canter, headed south down the highway.

Angus MacAuliffe did not so much as turn his

head to glance after him. "His name is Paul—John Paul," he growled. "Haven't I had suits made by his brother, the tailor in Fredericksburg, who croaked and died a matter o' months since? Now he comes, this—this common sailor. And plays heir, doubtless, for whatever the draper laid by. And then adds a new name. So as to appear a gentleman!" he snarled, and interrupted himself with a hiccough. "A gentleman, a Virginia gentleman, sir!"

He seemed to recall Noah's identity, as if he had known but forgotten. From Noah his glance traveled to Lady, the sorry-looking mare standing with the plow and swishing her tail at the flies and now and again twisting her neck to bite at them pestering her sore shoulder.

Angus MacAuliffe's fierce gesture almost threw him from his unsteady seat.

"You!" he roared at Noah. "Why stand there wastin' the day? Do I keep and feed ye to la-de-dah about with your betters?"

"Uncle," Eileen said uneasily, "shall you and I—"

"Wastrel!" the planter flung at Noah. "Are ye waitin' there to be twenty-one? Ye obstinate stick of a bound-boy, to work with ye!"

"Sir, I was but giving the mare rest," Noah explained. "Her poor shoulder is raw from the harness, it's so patched and—"

Angus MacAuliffe's bellow drowned his words.

"Poor shoulder, is't? My harness isn't good enough, eh?"

With a considerable effort he heaved himself out of the saddle, swaying as he reached the ground but hanging on by his horse's mane to steady himself. Then he flourished his short whip at Noah, who ignored it and started toward the plow.

"The mare's for work!" MacAuliffe bawled. "And so, by the Great Jehovah, are you!"

Noah's back crawled at the feel of the man close behind as he climbed the fence. But he did not look around. Reaching the mare, he examined her sores again, and a muscle quirked in his cheek. Then he sensed his master at his elbow and next instant felt stubby fingers dig hurting into his shoulder and yank him aside.

"Too hurt for plowing, do ye think? This worthless bag o' bones?"

"Please, Mr. MacAuliffe," Noah blurted out, "the horse is unfit. See her legs, sir, how they shake with weariness. See the rawness of her shoulder. I've tried to make the harness sit easy, but here—" He showed the rudely patched collar. "It rubs despite all I can contrive. With your permission, sir, mayn't I put her to rest and perhaps use one of the other horses to finish—"

"*No!*" The planter's wrath flushed his countenance yet redder. "Ye asked last night and I denied ye.

Are ye presumin' now to hand me advice? Eh? Ye need a lesson—both you and the beast. And gad, sir, here is yours!" Angus MacAuliffe cried, and brought his whip down hard across Noah's shoulders.

Pain as from a knife-cut sprang alive under the sleazy shirt Noah wore. But he had anticipated the blow and kept himself under control. His face set with contempt, he gave back stare for stare.

Calmly he said, "Give me the mare's lesson too, Mr. MacAuliffe. She can't stand more, she's that ready to drop. And I hate your bloody, senseless cruelty!" he exploded.

With his arm upraised to strike the plow horse, MacAuliffe paused, amazed. Then with an oath he struck.

Noah thrust out to divert the blow from Lady. But he was not quick enough, and the whip landed with a sticky sound fair on her raw, matter-moist shoulder.

What happened then was as swift as it was unexpected. Almost as if Lady, like Noah Carr, had borne all the evil she could of Angus MacAuliffe and cared naught for consequences, she reared up, snorting. The last flimsy strap around her chest snapped, leaving her free of the plow. Then her forefeet thudded down and her head swept low between her knees and her hind feet struck out savagely.

"You Need a Lesson," Shouted MacAuliffe

Impulse had made Angus MacAuliffe dodge at the horse's sudden movement. But in his unsteady condition, and what with the roughness of the plowed furrows, he toppled off balance. As he fell, one of the mare's heels struck hard to the side of his head.

It made a sickening thud. His hat snapped away as if jerked by a string. The planter's hands dropped like weights, and his whip fell. He swayed, eyes closed, then pitched heavily full-length on the turned-over ground.

He lay still.

Utter dislike for him ebbed away in Noah Carr's breast. He wrenched his look to Eileen as with a frightened moan she came clambering over the split-rail fence. Handicapped by her full green skirt, she nevertheless ran across the loam to her uncle, dropped on both knees beside him, and clutched his shoulder.

"Uncle Angus!"

She half-turned with an appealing glance upward. "Noah! Noah—is he dead?" she whispered.

CHAPTER TWO

PUNISHMENT WITHOUT MERCY

Noah stepped over the recumbent MacAuliffe and knelt on his other side. He felt the man's pulse, which was slow and faint. Gently he turned MacAuliffe's head, frowning at sight of blood oozing from an ugly hoof-cut and making a red streak from the upper jaw across the temple.

"We've got to have something to bind his head tightly. Then we must get him home," Noah said.

Eileen, on her feet now, stood molding her hands nervously. Looking up, Noah fastened his eyes on the long silken scarf knotted loosely at her throat and tucked inside her green riding jacket.

"Can we use that?"

Hurriedly she took it off and handed it to him.

As he sought to wind it around the hurt man's head, Zel, the groom, came up. From his waiting place ten yards from where the group had stood beyond the fence, the Negro had seen it all. Slightly crippled since a childhood accident, Zel scrambled nimbly over the fence and hobbled near. He knelt where Eileen had knelt, snatching the shapeless remnant of hat from his graying wool. Zel's eyes rolled in horror.

"Lawdy, Massa Noah! Is he—daid?"

"No. Lift his head, Zel. Dig your hands under—never mind a little blood. Now lift him. Gently! I'll wrap this scarf as tight as I can—

"There," Noah went on as he knotted the scarf. He leaned back, examining his work. Feeling MacAuliffe's pulse again, he found it somewhat stronger. But the planter still gave no sign of returning consciousness.

Noah reflected a moment. He rose, and going to Eileen, grasped her arms and looked at her searchingly. "Try not to give way. Can you get back on your horse and ride to the house and tell the servants to get ready?"

Her lips quivered. "Y-Yes."

He accompanied her a few steps, until he saw she was not too shaken to proceed alone.

"Don't worry over-much. He's had a very hard blow but I doubt it will be fatal. But hurry to the house," he instructed again.

Turning back, he said to Zel, "I wonder if we can get him on his horse? It would take too long to bring a wagon. It'll be hard hoisting him over that fence, of course." A thought struck him. "Zel, help me to pull the fence apart yonder. Then we'll lead his horse through."

"Yassuh, Massa Noah! We kin do dat!"

The two of them lifted rails and swung them sideways, working quickly until they had made an opening. Zel hobbled to MacAuliffe's mount, calmly nibbling shoots of grass. The Negro led the horse close to where his master lay while Noah stood calculating how to lift the insensible man into the saddle.

"We'll have to carry him together. We can't lay him face-down over the saddle," he reflected, "or he'd bleed too much. Let's pick him up, Zel. Gently!"

Angus MacAuliffe's weight proved a burden even for the two of them. As they neared the horse with him, it shied away, and Noah realized that he must hold the planter while Zel held the horse and guided MacAuliffe's leg over the saddle. For a moment he found himself straining every sinew with his master's full weight in his arms; but Zel quickly thrust MacAuliffe's right leg over the saddle, then shared the burden and with Noah heaved it higher. Their arms ached but somehow they pushed MacAuliffe to a sitting posture, from which he at once spilled limply forward on the horse's neck.

Noah held the unconscious man while he and Zel stood panting. "I'll have to mount behind him, else he'll topple off." Quickly he did so while the Negro held MacAuliffe. "Leave Lady where she is till someone can come and fetch her. You mount, Zel, and ride close to me and help hold him."

"Yassuh. But hit be mighty hard on him, Massa Noah. Maybe he can't stand de ride. Maybe Massa

M'cAuliffe gwine be daid when we gits to de house!"

"I don't know any other way. Let's hurry!"

Zel guided the burdened horse through the gap in the fence; then mounting his own animal, he came back. The two rode close at a walk, starting for the mansion more than half a mile distant, the red rooftop of which now and then showed through the trees.

In the twenty minutes required for the ride, Angus MacAuliffe stirred once or twice, moaning and mumbling unintelligibly. The scarf around his head seemed to control the bleeding, Noah thought, though it could not halt it. On arrival at the house he was relieved to find Africa, blackest and most powerful of the field hands, waiting with Boy Jed, who was a house servant, and Mammy Fanny and her two young daughters, who were maids.

"Done got the baid ready, Massa Noah," Mammy Fanny assured. "Lawsy, he look turrible! Y'all gwine fetch Doctah Salters foah Massa M'cAuliffe?"

"Yes. Can you boys take him? Hold his shoulders, Africa, so his head rests against your chest. Slowly! There—clasp your hands under his knees, Jed."

The two Negroes carried their master with no great difficulty, and, guided by Mammy Fanny, took him through the front doorway of the house. Noah looked around. He strode to Eileen's horse, held by one of the slave boys, and swung into its saddle.

"I'm going for the Doctor!" he called, wheeling the horse and giving it his heels.

Fortunately Doctor Salters had just returned home from making a call. After hearing Noah's message the physician shouted for his other horse to be brought for replacement of the mare now between the shafts of his two-seater buggy. In a matter of minutes he was on his way. Noah sat beside him, one arm thrust out to hold the reins of his mount trotting beside the rear wheels.

After he had given the details of the accident there was silence but for the crunch of wheels in the moist ruts of the highway.

Doctor Salters said reflectively, "Hard man to abide. Eh?"

Noah glanced at him. "Yes," he said briefly.

"Blame you for this, I cal'late. You should have killed the old plow horse with work and said nothing. Isn't your way, though. Eh?"

Watching the brown road ahead, Noah felt apprehension start in him. "I try to please him, Doctor Salters, but it seems like I can't. There are five years yet I must stay with Mr. MacAuliffe." He swallowed. "It sounds like a very long time."

" 'Tis. But you've got no choice." He urged his horse faster, then shot Noah a glance. "Unless," he pondered, "Mr. MacAuliffe would consent to your joining the militia. Raising militia everywhere these days. Fight for liberty. And if we want it, we'll have to fight for it. Hard," Doctor Salters said emphatically. "Hotheads on both sides bringing the issue on us rapidly. British wrecked Falmouth—like tossing a match in a powder barrel."

"Falmouth, sir?"

"Yes. New England. His Majesty's fleet swarmed in, shooting, pillaging. Burned the whole town. Thing like that starts a war, son. Continental Congress been warring with words this past year from their safe roost in Philadelphia. This year of Our Lord, 1775, will see real war with powder and ball. Any minute now!" Doctor Salters clipped out decidedly.

"Yes, sir. I understand there are resistance committees in all the colonies. Like Mr. Richard Henry Lee's Westmoreland Association, in which the members pledge not to buy English goods. Do you think, Doctor, that all thirteen colonies will hew together? Else isn't it madness to oppose His Majesty's army and navy?"

"Madness? Yes. But sometimes human progress leaps ahead in spells of madness. Patriot, myself," the physician announced bluntly. "Proud to stand with Mr. Thomas Jefferson, sir, and Mr. Patrick Henry—made a wonderful, fiery speech in Richmond! And that gentleman—Adams—from New England. Egad, and Mr. George Washington.

Slated to be general of armies we haven't got. Expect him to kill Redcoats with angry looks, I guess."

He shot Noah a look. "Bound-boy, eh? Like to be a soldier?"

Noah frowned. "I really don't know, sir. I doubt Mr. MacAuliffe would permit me to leave."

Doctor Salters turned his horse to enter the plantation grounds. Noah jumped out, and giving charge of the physician's horse and his own to a slave boy, showed the Doctor into the house. At sound of their entrance Eileen came hurrying down the staircase.

"He's still bleeding, Doctor Salters. And he hasn't become conscious yet."

"Don't fret, girl. Fretting's for old women that can't attract notice any other way." He mounted the steps two at a time and waited at the top for her. "Where is my gouty victim?"

She showed him into the sickroom, flashing Noah a worried look before she closed the door. He frowned, realizing there was nothing for him to do but await news. Then as he took to pacing slowly back and forth, listening for sounds within, the door opened and Zel came out.

At Noah's questioning look, Zel limped nearer. "Massa Noah, I don't think he gwine die quick, anyhow. Doctor, he gwine fix Massa M'cAuliffe."

"Is he conscious yet?"

"Not 'zactly. Miss Eileen say he dee-lirous. He talk crazy and I cal'late he don't really know what he say."

"Is that so, Zel? What did he say?"

Zel scratched his gray wool, looking uncomfortable.

"Was it about me?" Noah asked.

The Negro nodded. "He curse a lot and he say he sure gwine flog you, Massa Noah." Zel watched Noah's face. "Say he gwine flog you half to death."

There was a cold spot in Noah's breast. "I see," he said slowly. "Mr. MacAuliffe blames me, then, because Lady kicked him."

" 'Course he do. He don't ever blame himself, not dat man! Always ev'ything somebody else's fault. But I see it all, Massa Noah, and he hadn't oughter blame you." Zel sighed and spoke lower. "But I reckon, Massa Noah, y'all jus' about a slave, like me."

"It's about the same while my indenture term lasts," Noah sighed.

"Yassuh. But hadn't oughta be. You ain't really a slave. Y'all *really* like app-apprentice. That how bound-boy 'tended to be," Zel declared definitely. He shook his head. "Y'all been a gen'leman, Massa Noah, and you can read 'n' write 'n' do sums. Ain't no call to flog you. Hit ain't the law!"

"Mr. MacAuliffe is the law here, Zel," Noah grimaced.

They listened to loud talk in the sickroom. Although words could not be distinguished, Noah thought MacAuliffe was cursing and arguing with the physician. The talk quieted and presently Doctor Salters stomped out angrily. As Eileen followed, the Doctor paused in the doorway.

"Then kill yourself, if that be your stubborn way!" he shouted past her into the room. "But if you want to stay alive—*stay—in—bed*. Good day!" Turning, he nodded to Noah and stalked downstairs and out the front door.

Eileen, after seeing him out, returned up the stairs, merely shaking her head as she passed. MacAuliffe's growls came indistinctly until Mammy Fanny appeared from the sickroom. She waddled over to them.

"You no-'count, what you heah for?" she demanded of Zel. "Go 'long!" As he sheepishly took himself away, she added, "Massa gwine be all right, so don't get yo'self worrit-up 'bout nothin'." When Zel was out of hearing she turned to Noah.

"Dat man!" She jerked her head to indicate MacAuliffe. "No kickin' hoss gwine kill *him*." Her manner became protective, as it often did toward Noah. "He swear you make dat hoss do it. But Miss Eileen, she say he whip dat hoss on its sores till Lady git so mad she jus' kick out. Jus' the same, Massa promise he gwine punish you."

"Then Doctor Salters thinks he'll be all right?"

"If'n you think he *evah* all right!" She went on: "Dat man, all he care about is make people do his will. He don't have no joy from anything else. He say he own you, so he gwine flog you. Dat what he keep sayin'. But Massa Noah," she said earnestly, "you a bound-boy. You ain't a slave. Dey is diff'rent!"

He met her look. "Maybe Mr. MacAuliffe will forget when he feels better."

"Massa Noah, you always forgivin'. But he *never* feel better. He eat 'n' drink and his gout git worse and he git madder. 'Course now his haid done crack, the Doctah say. Maybe been crack for long time." She came closer, her hand on his arm. "Massa Noah, hit awful bad to git flogged. Special if you ain't got no meat on your bones, like you ain't. 'Course, I only a slave, so if Massa M'cAuliffe want flog me, I got to have it. There ain't *no* place in the world safe for me so he can't git me. Not till I daid.

"But you diff'rent," she said indignantly. "You only got to keep from him till you twenty-one. Pshaw," Mammy hinted, "dat ain't long!"

He gazed at her in surprise. "Do you mean—"

"I ain't say nothin'," she interrupted defensively. "But s'pose you git flogged once. He see it easy, so he flog you again, and again. But hit gits worse'n worse for you. And you only a boy. You ain't got your growth."

"He Say He Gwine Flog You!"

She patted his shoulder. "An' you a good boy, I don't keer *what.*" She watched him significantly, then waddled down the stairs.

After a while he took himself outdoors. Zel, he saw, was bringing Lady in from the field, so he followed them to the long, low barn. For an hour he worked on the mare's shoulder sores, gently applying cloths soaked in brine to re-form the skin and toughen it. And all the while he worked he pondered the meaning of Zel's words and those of Mammy Fanny.

"Ain't no place in the world safe for me," Mammy Fanny had said. "But you diff'rent. You only got to keep from him till you twenty-one."

She was worried about the treatment he would receive if he stayed on here.

Many times Noah had thought of running away, when Angus MacAuliffe's vile temper made life almost unbearable. For MacAuliffe never was pleasant. Commonly, the man said little, sometimes passing several days without leaving the house. When he did emerge, looking flushed and sullen from prolonged drinking, he seemed bent on finding fault, picking a quarrel. Any trivial pretext would suffice to fire his temper and make him strike out with the handiest weapon. Everyone on the plantation was his potential victim.

Once, discovering Noah eating half a pie Mammy

Fanny had given him, MacAuliffe accused him of stealing it. For two days Noah was denied food and compelled to stand in the dining room, watching the fleshy Scot eat ravenously. At supper the second evening Noah, weak from field work, had fainted. Angus MacAuliffe roared with laughter.

There were other instances—many of them. Twice he had laid his whip across Noah's shoulders as he had today, and each time it had been all Noah could do to restrain himself from striking back. So he had taken to keeping out of MacAuliffe's way, avoiding his as much as possible. It was what the slaves did, but it was only partially effective.

In his heart Noah knew he despised the man—yes, hated him. He had never let himself think that before, but it was true. Indeed, it was doubtful if Angus MacAuliffe had a friend anywhere. Even Eileen, dutiful as she was, had no affection for her uncle, Noah felt certain. She was simply making the best of her stay until her father returned from Philadelphia and took her home with him to Edenton.

Noah sighed. "It's little use running away. He'd find me and punish me the more. He'd have the sheriff in every county in Virginia hunting me like an escaped slave," he muttered bitterly.

But to be flogged—and for an accident entirely the fault of MacAuliffe's own brutal tactics . . . Noah had seen a flogging once, and remembrance of it made him shudder. Sometimes when slaves were flogged too hard, they died.

His fists clenched. "I'll tell him he has no right to flog me! As a bound-boy I'm an apprentice, not a slave! There's a big difference, and he can't—"

He did not finish. Who would support his argument? What good would it do even to speak thus to MacAuliffe? It would merely serve to infuriate the man, make Noah's punishment the worse.

That evening as he sat on the veranda steps, Mammy Fanny summoned him. Noah rose and approached her in the doorway.

"Massa want you," she said.

Noah followed her up the stairs. His hand was on the knob of Angus MacAuliffe's bedroom door when Mammy's touch stayed him. He turned inquiringly.

"Massa Noah, you be keerful! I—I don't want you hurt none."

He managed a reassuring smile and entered the room. Eileen, in a chair at the bedside, turned to glance at him. Three brackets of candles placed about the room gave soft pools of light that showed MacAuliffe lying in the heavy mahogany four-poster bed. Bandages swathed his head and were tied under his chin, leaving only the long oval of his face exposed. His cheeks were flushed and his hawk-like gray eyes were feverish. There was a folded paper in one of his hands lying on the spread, and on the little table at the bedside lay one of Angus MacAuliffe's dueling swords.

At the sound of the door opening, he swung his eyes to Noah. There was silence in the room as Noah advanced to the foot of the bed, hat in hand.

"I hope you are feeling better, Mr. MacAuliffe?"

Silence continued. The piercing eyes seemed to stare into Noah's mind. When MacAuliffe spoke his voice was crackling and cold as ice.

"You meant to kill me. You tried to make that mare—"

"Uncle," Eileen begged. "Please don't excite yourself!"

He swung his look to her and she fell silent. Again the sharp angry eyes pinned Noah.

"I've had enough of your lazy impudence. Your good-for-nothing shiftlessness is bad enough, but when you try to put me out of the way—why, I could have you swung from the gallows!" Angus MacAuliffe burst out. "And, egad, perhaps that's what I ought to do!"

He rushed on: "No. That would be too good for you. Besides, I mean to teach you your place." He paused. "Noah, you are thoroughly bad. Do you hear?" he cried. "Don't stand there like a—a spineless lout, even if you are one!"

"I hear you, sir. And I—well, I don't think I am bad, sir. I've worked hard for you, Mr. MacAuliffe. I've always tried—"

An oath cut him short. MacAuliffe had jerked to a sitting posture. Moaning as the movement brought a twinge of pain, he clapped both hands to his head. Noah waited. The man dropped his hands and clutched the paper lying on his knees.

"You dare to defy me! I'll flog you within an inch of your life! Do you hear? I swear I'll do it!" He tapped the paper. "I'll remind you you're but a miserable bound-boy—it's all written down here, my rights and duties. By heaven, I'll prove to you impudence doesn't—"

"Sir, I am a bound-boy. But I'm no slave. You haven't the right—" Noah began.

With an oath that made Eileen start from her chair Angus MacAuliffe whipped back the bedclothes and swung his feet to the floor. Snarling, he reached for his sword lying on the night-table as he swayed to his feet.

"Uncle! Please, Uncle!" Eileen cried.

Her attempt to reach the sword before he did failed. Eileen retreated a step. MacAuliffe, mouthing curses like a man possessed of Satan, lurched erect. His glittering eyes ignored the girl.

"I'll—run—ye—through!" he panted, and lifting the sword came straight at Noah.

CHAPTER THREE

THE FUGITIVE

Eileen shrank away, a hand at her throat. Then, thinking only of Noah's danger and heedless of her own, she flung herself at her uncle. Too late his attention swerved to her and surprise at her daring mingled with the ferocity of his look. Noah, striding around the foot of the bed, felt a clammy hand of horror squeeze his heart as Eileen jerked when the point of the blade struck her sleeved upper arm. Steel reappeared through the cloth as Eileen cried out in pain.

Fury flooded Noah then. Stepping around the girl, he seized advantage of Angus MacAuliffe's amazed hesitation at what he had done. Noah's sinewy fingers shot to the man's fleshy throat. With his other hand he ripped the sword from the planter's grasp, meanwhile thrusting with his left to fling the man back onto the bed.

Then, his eyes blazing, Noah lifted a knee and brought the sword down on it, snapping the blade in two. He hurled the bits to the floor. For an instant he stood panting, eying MacAuliffe as if he might pounce on him and strangle him. The paper lying on the bedclothes caught his attention—the indenture by which his mother had given him into Angus MacAuliffe's control until he should become of age.

Noah snatched it up. His eye caught a glimpse of red ribbon fastened by a gold seal, and of heavy black script down the length of the sheet. In a flash he had ripped the paper in two—then hesitated. On impulse he stuffed the pieces inside his shirt. He looked again at MacAuliffe and found the man's eyes closed as he lay breathing hard, unconscious.

Noah turned to Eileen. As he did so the bedroom door burst open, and Mammy Fanny and Zel pelted into the room. Mammy's eyes went to MacAuliffe, then to Noah, then to Eileen. Sight of the deepening reddish stain on the girl's sleeve brought hands clasping over her bosom in a prayerful gesture.

"*Lawsy!* Miss Eileen—you're kilt!"

Eileen swayed. Noah caught her as she fainted. He lifted and carried her around the foot of the bed, past the thunderstruck Zel and the frightened Mammy Fanny, and out of the room. In the corridor he hesitated. Zel plucked his sleeve, stammering and pointing. In another moment Noah had followed him into Eileen's bedroom two doors down the corridor, and laid her gently on her bed.

He straightened. "He came at me with the sword, but Eileen tried to stop him. He stabbed her!" he explained.

Mammy Fanny elbowed him aside. She held

smelling salts under Eileen's nostrils and almost at once the waxen eyelids fluttered with evidence of returning consciousness. Mammy Fanny handed the salts to Noah and waddled swiftly to the pitcher of water standing in the white bowl on the washstand. In another moment she was tenderly bathing Eileen's wound.

Noah stood grappling with confused thoughts. Zel, who had darted away for a hasty glance at MacAuliffe, came trotting back.

"He act like he daid," Zel reported frightenedly. "Only he breathin'. Like a wind-broke hoss."

"There." Mammy Fanny straightened up from Eileen's side. "You jus' lie quiet, honey. You' arm ain't hurt real bad. Hit jus' prick you, like. You gwine be all right, chile."

Eileen, despite Mammy's protest, sat up. Her face was pale and her eyes shone with slow-ebbing excitement. She touched her shoulder where Mammy had turned back her short sleeve and applied a bandage. Then she saw Noah.

She got to her feet quickly, steadied by Mammy Fanny. "Oh! Wasn't he frightful?" A shudder ran through her.

It made anger flame up in Noah, anger that he had been fighting to control. "I ought to have killed him. I ought to do it now!" He half-turned to leave the room.

"No!" Eileen flew to restrain him. "But—he may kill *you.* He'll never get over this, and—" She watched his face fearfully.

"I can't stay here. I've tried my hardest, but I—I can't!" Realization of how true this was swept over him. "I've got to leave."

"Yessuh!" Zel agreed emphatically. "Dat man skin you alive 'f you around when he git better. Y'all jus' can't stay here, Massa Noah. But where y'all gwine go to git from he reach?"

" 'Course you can't stay." Mammy Fanny waddled nearer. "Zel, don't you ask Massa Noah where he gwine go. 'Cause Massa M'cAuliffe, he gwine ask you, and he gwine ask me, 'Where dat boy now?' And we best not know so we can't tell. Massa Noah," she declared earnestly, "hit don't matter where, jus' so you *go.* Any place better for you than here. And you only got five yeahs," she reminded. "You keep from his way till you git to be a man. Massa M'cAuliffe, what he gwine do to you then?"

She turned to Zel. "You see how is he. Close and lock his door and bring me the key. Gwan, now!"

Zel hurried away. Noah walked up and down, thinking. It was a serious thing, he well knew, to flee indenture. Angus MacAuliffe would spread his description far and wide, and anyone recognizing Noah could collect a reward for turning him over to authorities. And if MacAuliffe got him back by such a means he would be entitled to punish him severely. He would get a flogging, of course, perhaps more than one. His life would be worth little—nor would anyone in Virginia so much as question Angus MacAuliffe if his bound-boy died from severe beatings.

The law was entirely on the side of the master. Indenture, originally devised to resemble apprenticeship, actually was much like slavery except that it ended at a certain age, usually twenty-one. Negroes like Mammy Fanny and Zel must remain slaves all their lives unless given their freedom—a rare thing indeed.

Eileen watched him tensely. "I'd better start now," Noah said.

Zel returned with the key to MacAuliffe's bedroom, which he handed to Mammy Fanny. Some signal passed between them, and Zel faced Noah.

"Massa Noah, maybe we don't see y'all no more. So I got to tell you, I with Massa M'cAuliffe when your mammy sign you for bound-boy."

Noah gave an exclamation. "I don't remember you there in Norfolk, Zel."

"No, sah, but I was. You stay in one house while your mammy sick with typhoid in 'nother. Massa M'cAuliffe, he like frien' to your mammy, and go to see her. I waited right at the doah of the sickroom, and I hear dem talk. Only I can't hear everything dey say. But I know dis—your mammy, she act like she know Massa M'cAuliffe for long time. And he act smooth 'n' nice, not like he usually do, all grumpy. And dey talk, and Massa M'cAuliffe, he come to de doah and say, 'Fetch me ink.' So I do, and I see papers in dat room, and when I stan' at the door again I knew dey sign papers."

Zel paused for breath. "Den I hear Massa M'c-Auliffe tell yoah mammy, 'Dere, dat done, I take good care yoah boy, jus' like he my own. I see he git good book-learnin' and when he growed he gwine be fine Virginia gen'leman, and he nevah have to do labor.'

"Den," Zel continued, "we wait in dat house, and yoah mammy die next mornin'. Massa M'cAuliffe, he send me back heah, but he stay for the fun'ral, and when he come home you's with him."

Noah waited eagerly. Zel molded his hands, glanced at Mammy Fanny, then at the floor. Finally he said:

"What seem queer to Mammy Fanny and me is yoah mammy—she was a lady. I know dat from how people in dat house treat her. Den Massa M'c-Auliffe sayin' he gwine give you book-learnin' and you gwine be fine Virginia gen'leman. And mos' of all," Zel emphasized, "he say y'all never gwine do labor."

"Dat seem pretty queer," Mammy Fanny declared. "Massa M'cAuliffe ain't send you to school. You ain't gwine be no gen'leman if *he* fix it. You jus' bound-boy. And one thing more—" Mammy hesitated. "Sometimes when Massa M'cAuliffe speak about you when you ain't there, he call you 'dat brat.' "

"Brat?" Noah frowned.

The two Negroes exchanged looks. "Massa Noah, don't you know what is a brat?"

"No-o."

"Dat a chile ain't got no pappy. You know yoah pappy?"

He shook his head. "Mother always said she'd tell me more about him some day. But I believe," he said slowly, "Mother and Father ran away from home very young and were married. They came from England, you know. They went to Trinidad and—" He shrugged. "That's all I know."

They started at the sound of pounding in another room, and knew that Angus MacAuliffe had regained consciousness. Eileen, with fright again in her eyes, seized Noah's wrist.

"If you're really going—? You'd best make it at once!"

"I take care dat man," Mammy said grimly, meaning MacAuliffe. "Zel, you fix sandwiches 'n' things for Massa Noah—an' you hurry 'bout it too. And get them pants 'n' jacket we save for him." To Noah she explained, "We always know you can't stay heah till you twenty-one. So we git things ready-like. But you better go quick," she urged at the sound of renewed pounding accompanied by muffled shouts.

Zel darted from the room and Mammy Fanny waddled after him. She stopped in the doorway, a sad, affectionate smile on her face.

"Good-bye, Massa Noah. You always be good boy like you been heah. An' don't let dat debbil catch you! An' I hope—" She swallowed and her eyes grew misty. "I hope Zel'n me see you again foah we all meet 'n Paradise with de heavenly Lawd."

She was gone.

Noah's eyes met Eileen's. She offered her hand, which he clasped in both of his. There was a moment's hesitation.

"Don't let him catch you, Noah."

"No," he promised.

"I—hope we'll meet again. Would it be safe for you to write me a letter home in Edenton? I'd like to know how you are, Noah."

"Yes, I'll write. It wouldn't have been livable here the last two months without you." He gulped and gave her small, warm hands a last squeeze. "Good-bye, Eileen."

Turning, he strode from the room. In the corridor he paused, and the ghost of a smile came to the

Noah Took Her Hand in Both of His

corners of his lips as he heard Mammy Fanny boldly scolding Angus MacAuliffe and apparently forcing him back in bed. Then Noah hurried down the stairs and made his way through the silent plantation house and out the rear door to the kitchen in a separate building close by.

Twenty minutes later he reached the highway, carrying a parcel of food in one hand and wearing the best of his much-patched shirts, and the jacket and trousers Mammy Fanny had kept hidden for the time she knew Noah would need them. Far from being new, they were nonetheless better than he usually had. They had been MacAuliffe's, as Zel chucklingly acknowledged, until Mammy Fanny caused them to disappear and be forgotten.

Noah paused, looking back at the mansion. It loomed a ghostly white in the light of myriad stars and a crescent of moon. Yellowed windows in the room above the veranda proved that Mammy Fanny and perhaps Eileen were ministering to MacAuliffe. Shadows spilled darkly along the front and side of the house, and the outbuildings and distant Negroes' homes were lost to view.

Noah drew a long breath. He glanced this way and that along the road. Which direction should he take?

He decided on the highway to Fredericksburg, which lay mainly northward on his left. There was no city within several days' walk the other direction, and Noah thought perhaps it would be easier to lose himself amid many people than in open country. At any rate, he had to start for some destination and Fredericksburg would do.

He walked rapidly for a mile, then slowed lest he soon tire at this pace. It seemed so strange to be leaving Angus MacAuliffe behind, so daring! Yet with every passing half-mile Noah seemed to feel lighter. It was as if a heavy burden were slipping from his shoulders, pound by pound. He discovered himself whistling, but broke off lest some late-night traveler notice him and stop to talk.

But it did buoy him up to realize that with every step he left Angus MacAuliffe and his petty, hateful ways farther behind. In the cool night, with the stars winking down at him in milky friendliness, Noah for the first time in many, many months felt almost happy. Because he was leaving his old miserable existence for freedom.

"Freedom," he mused aloud, and stopped.

That was what so many folk were talking about. Freedom for American colonists oppressed by masters far across the sea in England. Freedom was what had drawn men together in the First Continental Congress in 1774, and now in 1775 in a second. There would have to be fighting aplenty to gain freedom, warned leaders like Mr. John Adams of

Massachusetts and Mr. Patrick Henry of Virginia.

Wasn't Noah at this moment fighting for his own freedom?

He resumed walking, his eyes squinting thoughtfully. Something had made him remember Mr. John Paul Jones, who had been master of vessels in many foreign seas.

Noah's eyes sparkled. "If I but stay out of Angus MacAuliffe's clutches," he told himself, "I can do anything I wish. Maybe—it *could* be—that I shall become a sailor!"

CHAPTER FOUR

TALK OF AN AMERICAN NAVY

The Virginia House, the leading hostelry of Fredericksburg, was doing a thriving business that evening. Its proprietor, a little red berry of a man, lively as a bouncing ball, ran hither and yon looking after his guests. With the expertness of long experience at inn-keeping he aided friends to find each other and those who bore hostility—especially in political matters—to avoid collision.

From the taproom with its dark oak walls and gleaming copper spigots, Calvin Frenewell bounced to the adjoining supper room where half a tree trunk blazed in the great fireplace. Greeting guests, speeding service, solving problems whispered by his staff, Good Host Frenewell—as George Washington once had called him—dispensed the hospitality for which he was famous.

"Here, you! Boy!" Frenewell called.

Noah Carr, bearing a tray laden with roast guinea fowl, veered his course toward the innkeeper. Frenewell took the tray from him, hailed a Negro, and gave orders where to deliver it. Then, inclining his head for Noah to follow, he bounced toward the carriage-yard door.

He paused in the vestibule where they were alone. "Now," said Frenewell. He tapped Noah's chest. "Ye been here a month, which is longer'n most of my help stays in these unsteady times. Ye been a willing enough hand, too. But what I want to know—" he kept tapping Noah's chest—"are ye a lad of discretion? Eh? Can ye keep your lips tight so no flies get in? Or out?"

"Yes, Mr. Frenewell, I can."

The innkeeper glanced over his shoulder as if to make sure no one overheard. "Well, I'll put ye to the test very quick. Ye know Mr. Patrick Henry when ye see him? He's been here oft of late."

"Yes, sir."

"And ye know Mr. John Paul Jones?"

"Yes, sir, I do."

"And Mr. Thomas Jefferson, eh?"

"I've seen him once, sir. But I think I'd know him."

"And Doctor Read?"

Noah nodded.

"And Mr. Joseph Hewes of North Carolina?"

Noah shook his head. "I don't believe so, Mr. Frenewell."

"Well, he'll come with one of the others—Jones, maybe. Now mind, I want ye discreet." Tapping Noah's chest, the innkeeper lowered his voice. "These gentlemen will be gathering anon. Mr.

Henry is already here. I showed him myself to the upstairs parlor." Frenewell hesitated, scratching in the sparse hair of his pink dome. "I never inquired right out your politics," he hinted.

"Sir," Noah returned promptly, "my sympathies are not with His Majesty!"

Frenewell nodded approvingly. "Good! Nor mine. Well, now. These gentlemen will be gatherin' in the upstairs parlor. You're to stand outdoors and receive 'em. As they arrive, escort 'em up by the outside staircase. It's a serious conference they plan. Mind," he cautioned, still tapping Noah's chest and gazing up at him earnestly, "don't get mixed up. Keep the gentlemen from general view all ye can. Do you understand?"

"Yes, sir."

"Serve 'em whatever they want. But do't quietly. You'll serve no one else. Don't be puttin' your ear to the keyhole, but stand ready outside the door. When they finish, early or late, show 'em down the outer staircase to their carriages and horses. Do ye grasp what's wanted?"

"Yes, sir. Good service. And most of all, privacy."

"Correct. You're a good lad or I wouldn't trust ye with this for 'tis important. There's somethin' brewin' that's not for you or me to know—but it's on our side. So we'll keep the gentlemen from collidin' with any red-nosed swaggerers wearin' His Majesty's scarlet coats. Eh?"

He scuttled away. Before the swing-door closed Noah heard him cry cheery greeting to newly-arrived British officers in the taproom:

"Ah, Colonel Swain! Fine to see ye, sir, and your distinguished staff. Make merry, gentlemen, the house is yours!"

Noah smiled as he went out in the carriage yard to await the men he was to serve. Calvin Frenewell possessed quick wit and good sense, as indeed a successful innkeeper must in these times. For political matters were fast heating to a boil in Virginia as everywhere else in the colonies. Men who considered themselves "Patriots" every day flouted more openly the authority of His Majesty, George the Third of England. The British troops quartered in many larger towns were contemptuous of these "freedom-lovers" and sneered at them, trying to provoke fights which the well-armed soldiers stood to win. Those colonists—called "Loyalists"—who supported the King had ceased speaking to Patriot neighbors save to quarrel. It was an explosive situation, due any moment to blow up in a war of rebellion against the Crown.

The King's officers suspected the Virginia House, a famous gathering place, as a scene of Patriot plotting. Hence Colonel Swain and his staff frequented the inn, trying to uncover treason; and this explained

Calvin Frenewell's anxiety about the conference tonight. Frenewell, heart and soul with the Patriots' cause, nevertheless had to stay friendly with Loyalists and soldiers in order to keep the peace. And he was shrewd at steering a middle course, Noah reflected.

It was a month now since Noah had fled the plantation of Angus MacAuliffe. Perhaps he was reckless to remain in Fredericksburg when he would be safer from capture in Richmond, say, or better, in far-off Philadelphia. And he intended to remove now, soon. But Calvin Frenewell had treated him well, seeming to suspect something about his past though he asked no questions. When he came on Noah hiding in the scullery while the Sheriff lounged in the taproom, Frenewell's little blue eyes had narrowed and he said:

"Have your head shaved tomorrow, lad. It changes one greatly. However," he said, "in your present dress ye could pass for someone else than the ragamuffin ye were when ye came."

And that; Noah thought, was true. His hair had been cropped off and his garb was the livery of the Virginia House. He wore a red stocking cap that made his ears prominent, and a black coat, a yellow weskit, tan breeches, white stockings, and shoes with bronze buckles. They were, indeed, the best clothes he'd known since his indenture to Angus

MacAuliffe.

But he must leave the Virginia House soon. Angus MacAuliffe, he'd heard a guest tell another, was nearly well. "A bound-boy struck him on the head with a rod," the man said. There was always a chance of his visiting the inn, for now and again he came to Fredericksburg. So, much as he regretted thought of leaving his good employment with Mr. Frenewell, Noah had made up his mind to ask for his pay in a day or two and be off.

"If Angus MacAuliffe captured me, he'd beat me to death!" he reflected with an icy sensation in his stomach.

A carriage rolled into the yard and Noah hastened to it. A Negro boy ran from the stables to take the horse as two men alighted.

"Good evening, gentlemen. Doctor Read?" Noah inquired.

"Yes. And you?"

"Mr. Frenewell ordered me to take you to your room, sir. Mr. Patrick Henry is waiting," Noah added, to convey that he knew why they had come.

"Ah. Come along, Hewes. We want this private, lad. You understand?"

Noah led the way up the outside staircase and presently was showing them into the second-floor parlor. Mr. Henry, a slender, black-haired gentleman, thrust his steel-rimmed spectacles onto his high forehead as he rose from some papers spread out on the table. Doctor Read, who resided in near-by Goochland County and was a neighbor of Mr. Henry, greeted him and shook hands.

"Do you know Mr. Joseph Hewes? He is owner of several ships in Carolina as well as a member of the Continental Congress. I assure you Mr. Hewes's knowledge of naval affairs—"

A mute sign from Mr. Henry made Doctor Read glance at Noah. The three men stood silent as Noah closed the door and returned to the yard. None too soon, either, for he recognized the short figure with wide, powerful shoulders just dismounting and giving his horse to the boy.

"Captain Jones?" Noah said. His pulse hastened as he wondered whether he would be recognized.

"Mr. Jones, if you please. Can you take me to meet—certain friends?"

"This way, sir. Some of the gentlemen have already arrived."

As they reached the candlelit second-floor corridor Noah determined to test recognition. He stood so the light fell across his face. Mr. Jones's pale blue eyes pinned him, moved away—came back to Noah. About to knock on the door, the mariner paused.

"Haven't we met somewhere, young man?"

Noah felt himself perspiring. If he revealed himself would Mr. Jones turn him over to the sheriff?

He clenched his fists and swallowed hard.

"Your pardon, sir. In these mixed-up times there are oft sound reasons for not remembering faces. My own memory, sir, is a poor thing."

The faded eyes playing on him twinkled. "Your wisdom, lad, is less only than the improvement I observe in your health." He turned his back on Noah, rapped, and was admitted by Mr. Henry.

With a sigh of relief Noah returned to his post outdoors. John Paul Jones knew him, then. At least Mr. Jones felt sure he knew Noah, and perhaps actually recalled their few moments' talk with Eileen beside the half-plowed field. But there was no danger from him: of that Noah was certain. Nevertheless, if he could so readily be recognized it was more unsafe at the Virginia House than he had supposed.

"I'll leave tomorrow!" he vowed.

Mr. Thomas Jefferson, a tall, young-looking gentleman, soon arrived and was shown to the upstairs parlor. Distinguished, Noah thought him, with his plain but splendid quality clothes, and his well-powdered wig, and the ebony cane with the polished silver top that he carried. 'Twas a sword inside the cane, Noah had heard someone say. Mr. Jefferson had invented the contrivance. He had also invented a lift to hoist food from the basement kitchen at his home, Monticello, to its dining room—a thing called a "dumb-waiter." He was a remarkable man, talented in the law, farming, mechanics, and many another subject.

Taking up his station outside the parlor, Noah heard the hum of voices and now and again caught a word. But he could make little sense of it, and remembering Mr. Frenewell's caution, did not try to overhear what was intended to be secret. Presently the door opened and Doctor Read beckoned him.

"Some of us have not dined. Take the orders, boy. Bring me a pot of coffee that's fair boiling. And make no display," he warned, "whom you are serving."

"No, sir. Mr. Frenewell gave orders that you are to have good service and *privacy*, sir."

He took down the orders, feeling the interested gaze of Mr. Jones on him, then withdrew. When Noah returned with a heavily laden tray he knocked and was admitted. The men fell silent while he served them around the shining mahogany table. Except, as he was leaving, Mr. Patrick Henry declared angrily as if resuming interrupted talk:

"You say the people must be aroused, Mr. Hewes, and I subscribe. For 'tis the Rubicon we're all of us approaching. Boldly, with weapons flashing, we seek to cross—for liberty awaits on the other shore if we shall strike down our oppressors! But if we cavil and shake in fear of blood-letting, we shall fail.

There will be a dear cost, but either we must spend treasure and lives, or our honor and self-respect!"

"Mr. Henry's eloquence is a sharp weapon," quietly observed Mr. Thomas Jefferson as he poured a glass of sherry. "We have need of many more such. But we must also furnish weapons of hard steel to General Washington's troops. For the Redcoats may strike any—"

The door closed and Noah did not catch the rest. Or no—the door, he saw by a crack of candlelight, was not tightly shut. He reached for the knob, then hesitated. It was tempting to hear voices yet not words. And the fiery words of Mr. Henry made Noah glow inwardly.

He stood motionless.

"—arm General Washington's troops, 'tis true," came Doctor Read's brittle tones. "I am not one to spare treasure for that cause, my friends. And let's remember our long coastline as well. From northernmost New England past New York, Delaware, Maryland, and to the south end of Georgia we stand defenseless against the Royal Navy. Do ye forget Falmouth—how 'twas ravaged and burned? Think how His Majesty's troops are at this moment quartered in Boston! Why? For lack of protection. We must have it by sea, also, gentlemen!"

"It is an essential military aid to General Washington," agreed Mr. Jefferson in his rich tones.

"We Must Also Furnish Weapons of Hard Steel."

"Our visitor tonight, Mr. Joseph Hewes of North Carolina, is acquainted with marine matters," said Mr. Jones.

"No better than you, sir. Gentlemen," said Mr. Hewes, "I bring you word from Philadelphia and, further back in time, from Carolina. In my colony there is strong sentiment to equip privateers. There is weak sentiment to form a Continental Navy. But in Philadelphia a group of us reached the conclusion that the last step is the most desirable."

" 'Tis easier to grant letters of marque. They encourage private shipowners to send vessels to sea well-armed so as to capture rich merchant prizes." Noah thought it was Mr. Henry who spoke.

"So many persons believe. It is a strong appeal to men's pocketbooks. I myself am forming another view," said Mr. Jefferson.

"And I, sir!" warmly put in Mr. Jones. Noah heard a chair scrape, as if the mariner hunched closer to the table. "Can we expect private shipping to overwhelm thirty- and forty-gun frigates of the Royal Navy? Mind, gentlemen, where valuable merchantmen sail, there sail men-o'-war to protect 'em. In the words of Poor Richard:

'Vessels large may venture more,
But little boats must hug the shore.'

"In this instance, vessels large are those well-armed and manned by trained fighting crews," Mr.

Jones said earnestly. "The little boats are privateers, carrying a few guns and manned by money-seekers. They will not sail in squadrons under single command. They rove about, each for itself. Privateering, gentlemen, is but a weak crutch that will not support us in warfare with a great battle fleet!"

There was momentary silence. "Mr. Jones believes we must form a navy," said Mr. Hewes. "I heartily subscribe to this. Trained fighting sailors with the best weapons—that is our need. Will they not encounter trained fighting sailors with the best weapons?"

"But the expense!" objected Doctor Read.

"Where will we get the funds?" put in Mr. Henry.

"From the Continental Congress," declared Mr. Hewes. "True, the Congress has not yet heard this proposal and will not like its cost. But a few of us in Philadelphia have discussed this. We feel a navy to be as important as an army. If we are to battle the lordly frigates of His Majesty, then we—"

Rustling feet lost the remainder to Noah. He sighed, disappointed. For this *was* important, as Mr. Frenewell had told him. Perhaps a navy would be formed. Perhaps Mr. Jones meant to serve in it. And he would prove a staunch fighter, Noah had no doubt.

Doctor Read summoned him then, ordering a fresh pot of coffee. Noah hurried down the outer staircase, intent on missing as little as possible of this fascinating discussion. He started across the tip of the yard for the kitchen, aware that a carriage had just arrived but giving it no heed until someone roared:

"You—boy!"

Noah paused. Trained this past month to serve, he automatically responded with a stable-boy arriving to hold the two horses. Noah went to the carriage step, touching his forelock.

"At your service, sir."

"Well then, provide the service! Must we wait all night in your smelly courtyard before ye deign to see us? Well!" the man rasped. "Don't stand there like a graven image! Unlash the trunk from the rear! Show us to our rooms! Come alive or I'll lay my whip over your back," he threatened.

As the heavy-set man clambered out of the carriage, then assisted a slight girl to alight, his tones shivered through Noah like rasping edges of metal. He longed to flee but felt rooted to the ground.

For the girl was Eileen and the man was Angus MacAuliffe!

CHAPTER FIVE

TRAPPED

"Yes, s-sir. Will you kindly step indoors, sir? Mr. Frenewell will see to your comfort. I'll fetch the trunk by the back stairs. It will be in your room, sir." With a great call on his numb muscles Noah moved to the rear of the carriage.

"Take the trunk to the lady's room, not mine. And quickly!" Angus MacAuliffe escorted Eileen across the yard and indoors while Noah fumbled at the heavy straps holding the round-top trunk.

When the door closed behind them he straightened, panting. Perspiration stood out all over him and his heart thudded. Half-realized plans for escape jumbled in his mind with the burning question as to whether he had been recognized. But no, obviously he had not. Else MacAuliffe would have seized him and bellowed for help. His old master had been too intent on getting service to think of his missing bound-boy.

While he worked the trunk loose, Noah thought fast. Impulse kept tugging at him to start down the highway away from the Virginia House, putting miles behind him as fast as possible. Then, looking warily about, he decided against doing that, at least not yet. He had a month's pay coming to him. And there was no need for panic. Neither Eileen nor MacAuliffe had got a look at him there in the dark. He was reasonably sure he could avoid coming face to face with his master.

Besides, that glimpse of Eileen made Noah want to talk to her. And he disliked thought of leaving while the conference continued in the second-floor parlor. It seemed that formation of a Continental Navy was under consideration, and if one were formed, doubtless Mr. John Paul Jones would enter it. If that happened—

Suddenly he realized what had long been in the back of his mind. War was certain to come. Believing in the Colonial cause, he wanted to share in the struggle. If there was a Continental Navy, and Mr. Jones was in it, Noah wanted to serve there too.

He stood a moment half-smiling in the dark. Yes. That was exactly what he would do!

The Negro boy led the horses away, and with the carriage gone Noah was left with the trunk. No-o, he would not take to his heels at once. Though he must be cautious, for to be captured by Angus MacAuliffe meant the much-promised flogging. And if he survived the flogging, Noah knew that his life on the plantation would be thrice as miserable as before.

He lifted the trunk on his back and staggered

with it to the rear door of the inn. Of a passing waiter he asked what rooms had been assigned the new arrivals and was told their numbers. Noah trudged up the back staircase to the partial third floor. He halted on the landing, listening while carefully he determined MacAuliffe's room and Eileen's next to it.

Moving ahead, he paused before 317. MacAuliffe was not there, judging by the silence within. Noah moved on to 315, and putting the trunk down, knocked. A voice bade him enter. He swung the door wide, then grasping the trunk by its broad leather end-grip, raised it and backed into the room. Eileen was at a mirror removing her maroon velvet hat with the colorful feathers in it. Her little hands tossed looser the cascade of chestnut hair on her shoulders. Idly she looked into the candlelit mirror at the servitor bringing her trunk.

Their eyes met. Hers flared. She turned quickly. "*Noah!*"

He nodded, grinning. "You're no more surprised than I was down in the yard when I realized it was Mr. MacAuliffe braying for notice."

"Noah!" She came toward him. He pushed the trunk in a corner and straightened. "In heaven's name, why haven't you got farther away than this? Oh, Noah, I'm afraid for you!"

"Don't be," he said with more confidence than he

felt. He stepped to the door and gently closed it. "Where is he now?"

"Downstairs. I said I had a headache and perhaps would retire soon." Impulsively she touched his arm as if to prove he actually stood there. "Are you all right? What have you been doing? Oh, Noah, you mustn't let Uncle Angus catch you! He swears he'll run you through with his sword—and I doubt not he'd try!"

"I hope he has a new sword. The old one lost its point, if I remember," Noah chuckled. "I shouldn't enjoy being stabbed with a blunt blade. How is your cut, Eileen?" he recalled.

"It wasn't serious, though it hurt for a day or two. Why!" she breathed. "I can scarcely believe my eyes! But, Noah," she hurried on, "hadn't you ought to flee? 'Tis not safe staying where Uncle Angus is. Please don't be so reckless."

"No," he agreed, taking a chair as Eileen sank in another. "I surely don't wish to have my late master discover me. But once I saw you, I had to speak to you. And there's—well, something going on that I wish to know more about." He remembered that he must not be gone too long from the second-floor parlor. "How is everything at the plantation? Did Mr. MacAuliffe punish Mammy Fanny or Zel about my departure? And where are you bound?"

"No, he didn't punish them though he suspected

they had something to do with it. Lucky for you, Uncle Angus had such a fever that he was ill several days. So he didn't really discover you were gone until he felt better. And then he had such a blaze of temper that it made his head pain and he had to return to bed. It's been horrible there," she added with a little shudder. "At times I do wonder if Uncle Angus isn't—well—"

"Touched?"

She nodded. "I shouldn't speak thus of mine own uncle. But he has been so horrid to everyone. And I'm thankful that at last I can leave. Papa is on his way from Philadelphia and should be here tomorrow. I shall return with him to Edenton."

Mention of the city made Noah remember. "Do you know a Mr. Joseph Hewes?"

"Oh, yes, Papa does. He is a fine gentleman who lives in Edenton, and he owns ships in the West Indies trade. Mr. Hewes says King George never will restore our rights, and at Mecklenburg he was a leader in fashioning the North Carolina announcement of independence from England. He and Papa have tried to organize militia and raise arms and money to send to General Washington besieging Boston. But—"

She broke off. "Noah, you are a—Patriot?"

"And would I be a Loyalist? Mr. Hewes," he rushed on, "wants to have a Continental Navy. And it may be that Mr. Jones will be in it. And if he is —well then, I hope also to serve."

"La!" she exclaimed, her eyes shining. "If only I were a man so I could do something as gallant and win great glory! And Noah, I doubt not you will, in full measure. For I've seen you are a fighter," Eileen added, smiling.

She sobered again. "Did you know that Mr. John Paul Jones also comes from Carolina, in a way? And you must keep this secret," she cautioned, "but his name formerly was John Paul, I do believe."

Noah frowned. "Then when Mr. MacAuliffe said he had changed his name—that he had added Jones —he spoke truly? Remember, Eileen, that day I was plowing and you and Mr. Jones paused in your ride?"

"Yes, Uncle Angus did speak truly. But mayn't a man add a name? Is that changing it? At least, not so it deceives."

"But why should he do so?"

"I don't rightly know," Eileen admitted. "I have heard that Mr. Jones also was in the West Indian trade, though he didn't sail for Mr. Hewes, but out of England or Scotland. Mr. Jones stayed a long time, I believe, with Mr. Willie Jones of Halifax, who is a great man in North Carolina. And from what I've heard said, when he first came there he was plain John Paul, and when he left he called himself John Paul Jones."

"But why? He wasn't adopted, was he?"

"La, so many questions! Perhaps he wanted to honor his friend. Perhaps they felt like brothers." She paused. "There was something," Eileen said slowly, "about some trouble at Tobago when Mr. Jones was master of a vessel. Mayhap he flew in the face of the King's officers. For he is a Colonies man, you may fasten to that. And it couldn't be any sort of stain on his character, I'm positive. Not Mr. Jones!"

"Indeed not. There's something—almost great about him," Noah declared. "He seems a man born to command. When he looks at me he makes me feel—oh, I don't know. But I should like serving under him to fight the Jack Tars' frigates!"

"And you'd make a splendid sailor, Noah. What shall you be, a captain?"

He chuckled. "I fear I shall be seasick at first, for I was ill on my little sailing thus far. Besides, there's no navy yet," he reminded. "They are talking of having one, and Mr. Joseph Hewes seems to be a ringleader in urging it."

He paused. "Eileen, shall we not meet again? Ever?"

Her eyes fell. "I should be sorry if we do not, Noah. But if you are bound to be a sailor, and I'm returning to Edenton—"

"Still, a vessel may put into Edenton for fresh water and provisions."

She smiled a little. "That would be nice. And if it doesn't, Noah, you may write to me. That is, if you wish to."

"I will. And will you now and again write to me? Eileen," he went on, carefully drawing an envelope from inside his shirt, "do you recall I tore in two the indenture agreement between my mother and Mr. MacAuliffe? Then I took it away with me, and I have been examining it."

"You mean—?"

"No. 'Tis a true agreement, I fear, and specifies that on my twenty-first birthday the indenture ends, whereupon Mr. MacAuliffe shall pay me ten pounds sterling, provided my services have been satisfactory." He grimaced. "Can you see him admitting my services have been satisfactory? If 'twould cost him ten pounds?"

They both laughed. "But here." He showed her. "The signature is my mother's, I suppose. Only—but of course she was ill when she wrote it," he amended.

Eileen gazed at him, then looked where he indicated. "It says 'Martha Carr.' A pretty name, isn't it?" She studied the writing. "It does look a bit crabbed, as if she wrote a letter or two, then lifted the quill, then wrote another letter, and so on." She looked up. "What is your meaning, Noah?"

He shrugged. "Nothing clear in my mind. I left behind at Mr. MacAuliffe's or somewhere a very old letter my mother wrote to my father before they were wed. 'Twas a keepsake of mine. I was thinking this signature looked somehow different than her writing in that one."

Their eyes held. "But, Noah, surely–"

"Perhaps my memory is faulty. And I lost that old letter somewhere, so I can't be sure. But I never have been able to believe I was meant to be indentured, Eileen."

Once more she studied the signature on the indenture. The name "Martha Carr" was plain, if crabbed. At last, shaking her head, Eileen straightened.

"It must be her writing, Noah. It binds you. Unless you can prove trickery of some sort."

"Forgive me for being set in what is only my feeling–that I was raised to be a gentleman. Though–" he frowned–" 'Tis something of a mystery about my father."

He whirled, and Eileen gave a quick gasp. For heavy steps sounding along the corridor slowed approaching the door of the room in which they sat. Eileen, who held the torn parts of the indenture paper, dropped it on the chiffonier beside her as they rose, her eyes holding Noah's at sound of a knock.

"Eileen?" It was Angus MacAuliffe.

Noah's blood went cold. The girl's large, frightened eyes fastened questioningly on his as she took a step toward the door, then hesitated.

"Eileen! Are you there?"

She swallowed hard, glancing in panic around the room for some means of hiding him. Noah, spying the trunk he had carried here, strode to it.

"Yes, Uncle. Just a minute, please!" She dropped on her knees and worked with a key hung on a silken ribbon around her neck. Unlocking the trunk, she threw the lid back. Then gesturing for Noah to help, she picked up clothing and flung it to the bed. Between them, they had the trunk half-empty in a matter of seconds.

Noah stepped in and crouched. Gently Eileen lowered the lid. She spoke to her uncle as she went to the door and admitted him.

Noah heard him stride into the room. "You were retired?"

"No, just resting. I'd started to unpack," Eileen explained. "I must have fallen asleep."

"Well, we can still get something to eat, though they're none too gracious about offering. Seems that one of their waiters simply vanished within the hour. Can't locate him anywhere. He hadn't worked here very long, and one of the guests suggested he's a spy."

MacAuliffe Strode into the Room

"A spy? For whom?"

"How would I know?" Angus MacAuliffe replied irritably. "Well, child, get yourself ready and we'll have some dinner. It mayn't be much but it should stop the pangs of hunger till morning."

"Thank you, Uncle. But I—I don't believe I'm hungry. Why don't you just—"

"Not hungry? Of course you're hungry! What's that?" he asked sharply.

Eileen had noticed the indenture paper lying on the chiffonier and was trying to pick it up without attracting notice. At her uncle's sudden interest she managed a careless smile.

"It's just a paper someone left. Of no importance, I'm—"

"Let me see it."

"Oh, it's nothing, Uncle. I was going to throw it away and—"

Noah, crouched uncomfortably in the trunk, heard MacAuliffe's chair creak as he rose, heard him stride across the narrow room. "Give it to me!"

"But Uncle, it's—" Eileen broke off as if MacAuliffe had snatched the paper from her.

There was momentary silence while he fitted the two ragged pieces together. A series of oaths spilled startledly from his lips, making Eileen protest.

"Uncle! Please don't use such language when—"

"What!" he roared. "Language? I'll use language!

And maybe something sharper on you, misguided wench! I'll use a knotted rawhide on *him*, I promise you truly! Where is he?" he snarled. "Quick, girl, unless you want to be turned over my knee!"

"Wh-where? Who, Uncle?" she faltered.

"Noah Carr!" he roared. "He's been here—this paper the villain stole from me proves that! He's about, somewhere! You've seen him—talked to him, I doubt not. *Where is he?*"

CHAPTER SIX

THE EAVESDROPPER

Crouched in the trunk on a padding of the girl's pleasantly scented garments, Noah felt an impulse to fling back the top and step out to confront his master. For Eileen, he remembered, had not locked the trunk after he got in it. There had not been time to think of that.

He felt his hiding place give just slightly, as if some weight had been deposited on it. Then hearing Eileen's voice close, he realized that she had sat on the trunk lid in the hope of distracting attention from it.

"Please, Uncle," she said shakily, "why do you speak to me s-so?" Noah could picture her holding a lacy mite of kerchief to her eyes as if tears were coming.

"Speak to you? I'll speak to you!" He stomped about the room. From the altering tones of his voice Noah knew he was stooping to peer under the bed. "Oh!" he groaned. "I'm still dizzy when I lean over. Curse it!"

He stomped nearer her. "Come, young woman! Your father will like to know if you're helping a bound-boy to escape! Tell the truth now. Noah *was* here?" he demanded.

"Y-Yes."

"Go on! Where is he now?"

"Noah only came to—I mean, he brought my trunk in. Truly, Uncle, I was astonished to see him! I had supposed he would be far away. He spoke of going to—to New York," she invented.

"New York? You didn't tell me that before! You declared you had no knowledge where he meant to flee. Eileen," he promised, "your father shall hear of this!

"What else? Tell me every word exchanged between you," Angus MacAuliffe demanded.

"Well, a man brought in my trunk. And—when he straightened up, I saw that it was Noah. 'Why, Noah!' I said. 'What in heaven's name are you doing here?' And Uncle, he was astonished to see me. Evidently he had not recognized us getting out of the carriage in the yard. And that's n-nearly all, Uncle," she told him as if resisting frightened tears. "He's gone. How should I know where? And why should I ever expect to see him again?"

There was silence. MacAuliffe strode up and down. Noah heard him halt as if pondering. Then his steps came nearer, and for an instant Noah crouched tensely ready to raise the trunk lid and leap out to grapple with the man. But Eileen, he remembered, still sat on it. Better to wait and hope to the last possible instant . . .

Her cry of pain made him start. "Uncle! Please don't twist my wrist!"

"Tell me the truth—all of it!"

Evidently he twisted her wrist again, for she moaned. She had risen from the trunk but Noah knew the two stood close to it. "Oh, Uncle! You're hurting me!"

"What did that rascal tell you? Where is he?" MacAuliffe cried.

"Please, Uncle! Oh," she moaned, "how could I know where a bound-boy would go? I—he must have fled, knowing that you would find him, else. Oh, my wrist!"

Noah thought MacAuliffe released her, probably thrusting her away as he let go of her wrist, for he sensed that she again sat on the lid of the trunk. He crouched, boiling with anger. There was in him an urgent impulse to thrust Eileen away and step out of the trunk—for 'twould be a pleasure to work off in blows some of his dislike for the man!

But something warned him to remain where he was and without a sound. It was far better to go undiscovered. Once known, he would be at the mercy not only of MacAuliffe but of any others notified by the hullabaloo he would raise that a bound-boy who had fled his master was at large. There was no telling how many guests of the Virginia House might want to curry favor with Angus MacAuliffe, or at least win the reward he undoubtedly had offered for Noah's capture.

Perspiring in his closed hiding place, he waited.

"Maybe he's still about the premises." MacAuliffe seemed to move away. "Eileen, remain in your room until I return. Don't leave it for any reason. Do you understand?"

"Yes, Uncle," she returned meekly.

"I'll have a look around. There must be a chance—" MacAuliffe did not finish as he opened the door. "Should he return, Eileen, you keep him here. Talk. Don't let him leave!"

His steps faded. The door slammed.

At last Eileen rose, and going to the door, slipped its bolt. She returned and lifted the trunk lid. Noah rose, pausing to let circulation resume in his legs which had been cramped tightly under him. Their looks held. The girl's face was pale but there was a glint of triumph in her eyes.

Noah stepped out of the trunk. "Eileen, you were magnificent. I am far in your debt. Though you shouldn't have incurred your uncle's anger only for me."

"I despise him!" she flared. "I do despise him! If my worst enemy were in your place, Noah, I shouldn't let Uncle know of it. And you are by no means my worst enemy."

"Indeed, I'm your friend and want you mine." He glanced around. "But I must leave here at once. Mr. MacAuliffe will be returning. Explain," he grinned, "that you bolted the door against my possible return. Ah!" Noah picked up the two pieces of his indenture paper. "I get this back. In his wrath my master forgot to put it in his pocket." He found the envelope he had used before, and thrusting the papers inside it, stuffed it inside his shirt.

They looked at each other. "Where will you go, Noah?"

"Not out in that corridor," he grimaced. " 'Twould be my fortune to meet him coming up the stairs." He indicated the double windows. "I shall use that exit, and at once. Eileen," he said, taking both her hands, "I am grateful for your friendship and your assistance. And I'll write to you in Edenton."

"Yes, Noah. I do wish you very great fortune. And if you serve with Mr. Jones at sea, I know you will give a fine account of yourself and win great glory. La," she added morosely, "if only I were a man!"

He laughed. "Then I shouldn't like you half so much. And you couldn't be so pretty, either." He squeezed her hands and let them go. "Good fortune to you, Eileen." There was a little lump in his throat as he realized he might never see her again. "I hope you will find a good husband and be very, very happy."

Without looking back he went to the end of the room and gently thrust the leaded-glass windows wide. Peering out in the moonlit dark, Noah saw that the gable in which he stood looked onto a slanting roof down to the bulkier two-story part of the building. He should be able to inch cautiously down the incline, he thought, seize the gutters, then drop to the ground.

As he thrust a leg over the sill Eileen came close behind him. "Do be careful, Noah!"

"Yes," he promised, getting his other leg over. "Good-bye."

A rap on the door made her whirl with sucked-in breath. "Eileen! Have you got this locked?" demanded Angus MacAuliffe, trying the knob.

Standing on the roof, Noah closed the windows behind him. He watched through the glass as she crossed and unbolted the door. As MacAuliffe, red-faced and suspicious, entered, Noah stooped out of his view. Seating himself, he moved little by little down the roof, which he was alarmed to find more slippery than he had anticipated.

Gradually he lowered himself, trying to check the pull of gravity by his heels and flattened hands and his sitting posture. A skylight came into view as he passed the gable, and dimly through its accumulated grime Noah saw figures standing and seated. He frowned; then his face cleared. It was the conference to which he was supposed to be playing waiter.

Curiosity got the better of his desire swiftly to be gone from reach of his master. Changing course, he worked his way to the skylight. He made certain no one was looking out the window and quickly rubbed a clear spot on the glass.

It was Mr. Thomas Jefferson standing closest, his back turned. Mr. Hewes, a strong-looking man of near fifty, with thick gray hair, sat on Mr. Jefferson's right and next to him was Mr. Jones. On the left of Mr. Jefferson were Doctor Read and Mr. Patrick Henry. Maps and papers littered the oval table around which the men sat.

Pressing his ear and cheek to the glass, Noah could hear Mr. Jefferson's talk, though not every word. He was urging that each colony draw up a statement of independence from England, as North Carolina had done recently. By crystallizing sentiment thus in each of the thirteen colonies, he declared, the way would be prepared for a manifesto of independence by all the colonies acting as one united government.

"It is unity we sorely need," Mr. Jefferson pleaded. "Can Massachusetts alone defy the power of George the Third? Can Delaware? Or Virginia? And if they defy His Majesty separately, will not the King's armies isolate us one at a time and compel our submission? But if we strike as one strong arm, our sword will go deep!"

He thrust his coattails back and sat down. Mr. Henry was nodding stern agreement.

"The time is close upon us, gentlemen," he reminded, "when each colony must kneel in obedience to the tyranny we despise, else it must come boldly into the open and fight. Thus, I am in sympathy with Mr. Jefferson's proposal. Let us, by free and open decision, adopt thirteen manifestos of rebellion—"

"That is a strong word, Mr. Henry," interposed Doctor Read.

"Ours is a strong purpose, sir. As soon as every colony has stated its determination on complete divorce from His Britannic Majesty, then must all representatives to the Continental Congress sign a single such manifesto for all. That will show the King whether his stepchildren across the sea mean business!"

There was general approval. "May we return to the subject of a Continental Navy?" suggested Mr. Hewes.

"Your pardon, sir. Let us delay until our ordnance expert joins us. It should be but a matter of minutes.

"Meanwhile, gentlemen," Mr. Henry went on, "in which situation do we find ourselves? Most of us are English-born or of English descent. Now we accuse His Majesty of oppression, of regulation without conscience. Do we bear hate for that land from which we sprang?

"I think not," he answered himself. "Merely, we bear burning resentment against a Government which seems to regard America as a blood-sucking vampire contemptuously regards its victims.

"What succession of events have shaped our determination to throw off tyranny?" he proceeded. "The King, on coming to the throne in 1760, felt that 'his farms,' as he referred to the Colonies, must contribute more to his treasury. He sought thus to make us pay for his blundering war with France, and to enrich himself and his ministers, and to prove to us in America that we are unfit to regulate our own trade.

"Between '63 and '67 taxes were laid on sugar entering the Colonies, then on certain business transactions, and soon on lead, paint, and so on. We were forbidden to issue money. The Quartering Act required us to feed and lodge British soldiery here to enforce the very laws we despise. The iniquitous Tea Act laid a burden on us for the enrichment of the British East India Company. Later we were forbidden to purchase more land from the Indians, and officers were named to license trading with Indians. Customs collections began in all our ports. The Coercive Acts followed.

"All these laws are to our disadvantage," Mr. Henry complained. "We pay, but we do not share. We are governed from two thousand miles away, but we have no voice in that government.

"This unfairness has brought anger to a patient people," he declared. "In '70 the Boston Massacre saw Redcoats firing on unarmed men and boys. In '72 the men of Providence angrily set fire to a King's vessel hunting alleged smugglers in Narragansett Bay. In '73 the Royal Governor of Virginia forbade the House of Burgesses to meet. In the same year tax-weary citizens of Boston refused to pay the heavy tax on tea and flung a cargo of it into their harbor. In '74 our expansion westward was halted when the boundaries of far-distant Quebec were widened to the Ohio River.

"Abuse after abuse has been piled on us," Mr. Patrick Henry growled, pounding the table. "We have begged for righting of these many wrongs, and to what end? More indignities! We are denounced in the halls of Parliament as barbarians.

"Gentlemen," he ended earnestly, "our hour is struck. Let us march as one army against our powerful oppressor. Let us fight and win independence! And remember, we are not traitors. It is England which has been traitorous, to her own kith and kin!"

He sat down mopping his brow. There were murmurs of approval from the others. Noah, listening with fascination, felt the desire to clap his hands and could scarcely restrain a cheer.

He saw several heads turn and knew someone had knocked on the door. Mr. Hewes rose and going to it, slid the bolt back and swung it open. At sight of the man standing there Noah, with quick-caught breath, all but forgot to keep his tight grip on the window sill lest he hurtle down the roof to the courtyard below.

"Mr. MacAuliffe!"

Indeed it was Angus MacAuliffe, now being introduced to those of the conference whom he did not know. Noah suppressed his hard breathing and with ear again pressed to the windowpane, listened intently.

"—served as a Lieutenant in His Majesty's Navy. He was a recognized expert in naval ordnance," Doctor Read was informing the others. "Mr. MacAuliffe now is a well-known planter some miles south in this region; but he should be able to give us information on His Majesty's ships-of-the-line. And perhaps he can be of great service to our Continental Congress in forming our own fleet."

Noah saw Mr. John Paul Jones and Mr. MacAuliffe exchange greetings that were but lukewarm. He saw Mr. Henry mutely inquiring something of Doctor Read, who went on to the group:

"Naturally there is no question of Mr. MacAuliffe's sympathies, else he would not be here tonight."

"I was born in Scotland," MacAuliffe said shortly.

Joseph Hewes Admitted Mr. MacAuliffe

"We Scots have no love for English kings."

"Well, then, let's get to business," Mr. Hewes proposed. "Mr. MacAuliffe, we have discussed a Continental Navy to prey on English supply vessels along our coasts, and to wage battle with men-o'-war blockading our commerce. Of course, the Congress will decide on formation of a navy. But you can perhaps suggest what weight of armament we must have, and so on."

Angus MacAuliffe tamped his black briar pipe, then reached for a candle to light it. The others waited in expectant silence.

"I favor preying on English commerce close to England," Mr. Jones spoke up. "For this I suggest a few fast vessels, not too great in tonnage, but as well-armed as may be. We could throw panic into His Majesty's own cities by raiding 'em. Folk would set up a hue and cry for the British fleet to be brought home from America for protection. It seems to me," he told MacAuliffe, "such a plan would be cheapest, easiest, and most effective."

"I do not think so," promptly declared Mr. Patrick Henry.

Angus MacAuliffe looked around the circle of faces. He let bluish smoke trickle from his nostrils that always reminded Noah Carr of ugly nail holes in a pipe.

"Ye served in the Royal Navy?" he asked Mr.

Jones.

Noah thought he hesitated. "Yes. I was a midshipman till I learned there was no hope for advancement."

"Quite. Before ye went in the slave trade," MacAuliffe nodded.

Mr. Jones bristled. It was injurious to a man's social standing to be associated with bringing slaves from Africa, though blue-blood Virginia gentlemen were willing enough to buy and use slaves.

"I was a lieutenant in the King's service," MacAuliffe went on, as if to emphasize his higher rank. "I was in charge of mounting heavy guns on the new, heavy frigates. Fifty guns, some of 'em carry, sir. Forty and less, others mount. And ye think to oppose this force? With how many ships?"

"We cannot quickly build and train a navy equal to the King's," Mr. Hewes admitted. "That is why Mr. Jones urges raids on English shores by two, three, five vessels at a time. It is a tactic he believes is within our reach."

Frowning, Noah listened to the debate on the wisdom of attacking the English coast. It did sound a bold thing. The suggestion was warmly regarded only by Mr. Hewes, who declared its very boldness was its strength.

As the talk waxed hotter, Noah felt resentment at Angus MacAuliffe's presence in the conference.

True, the man was said to be an expert in naval matters; but need he show such lordliness toward Mr. Hewes and Mr. Jones? And since when was MacAuliffe heart and soul a Patriot?

Thinking back, he sought to recall statements by his master indicating strong sympathy with the Colonies. He remembered MacAuliffe belittling various attempts to wring justice from King George—but true, he spoke sarcastically about everything and everyone. Assuredly Noah would not have guessed MacAuliffe was a staunch Patriot. On the other hand, would he have dared to label the man a Loyalist?

"He never said openly which side he would fight on," Noah muttered, striving to recall his days on the plantation. "Faith, I don't see him as the fighting kind, in any case. But I'd have guessed he had more loyalty to the King than to the Continental Congress . . . "

The uncertainty disturbed him. Suppose Angus MacAuliffe sat in this conference while his real sympathies opposed its motives? But no, Doctor Read was an ardent Patriot. He would have been careful not to vouch for a man who could be dangerous.

"Nevertheless, I'm apprehensive," Noah told himself half-aloud. "I can't quite trust him. Not in a—"

He never finished. Forgetting the precariousness of his perch, he carelessly shifted position. His grasp on the ends of the windowsill failed, and for a panicky instant he swayed on the slanting roof, clawing for a new hand-hold.

With a tremendous effort Noah flung his weight forward lest he hurtle sideways off the roof to broken legs and arms in the courtyard below. His head and hands shattered the small leaded-glass panes of the skylight. His shoulders followed.

Head first, he plunged into the conference room.

Instinctively he dropped his head on his chest to strike the floor on the back of his neck and shoulders, like a tumbler. Turning a complete somersault, he felt darting pain as his heels struck the chair Mr. Jefferson was startledly thrusting back.

Every man had leaped to his feet. A circle of astonished faces stared at Noah lying flat on his back, dazed.

CHAPTER SEVEN

UNEXPECTED AID

"What's this!" Mr. Henry hurriedly pulled down to his eyes the spectacles he wore more than half the time on his forehead.

"We've been overheard!"

"An eavesdropper!" exclaimed Mr. Hewes. He peered at Noah. "Why, it's the lad who—"

"Isn't he our waiter?" Mr. Jefferson's notable dignity, ruffled but for a moment, had returned. He stood staring down at Noah. "Why such an unceremonious entrance when the door is available?" he demanded with a crisp, dry humor.

Some of the breath had been knocked out of Noah by his fall. Gasping, he scrambled to his feet, his eyes darting from face to face. He shrank back, fumbling with one hand behind him for the window as a wild plan was taking form in his brain to leap out of the window and risk the dangerous steepness of the roof. Angus MacAuliffe, farthest from him in the room, was the man he feared. The others were not his enemies, and they could be made his friends with the truth. But not Angus MacAuliffe!

His groping hand felt cloth and buttons. "No farther, lad," a voice suggested calmly. "We wouldn't want ye breaking your daredevil neck down that roof. At least till we've discussed matters a bit."

That was Mr. Jones. Noah spun around. He swallowed as his eyes met the icy blue of the other's. There was a pause. Then Noah saw recognition in the mariner's look, and thought the flowing lines from his nose to the corners of his straight slash of mouth softened a very little.

"Why enter so—er, tumultuously?" Mr. Jones asked. "I doubt not ye could have heard as much at the keyhole, and perhaps more comfortably."

This brought a short laugh from Mr. Jefferson. It seemed to release demands, exclamations, comments from the others so that for a few seconds everyone interrupted everyone else. Seizing an opportunity that would not be repeated, Noah whispered hoarsely:

"Mr. MacAuliffe, sir—I fled his plantation. In heaven's name, sir, don't—!"

If his words were run together, the appeal on his face seemed to reach Mr. Jones. The faded blue eyes bored deeper into him, yet were not hostile. Hope flared in Noah as he waited.

Fully an inch shorter, Mr. Jones reached out sternly and gripped his shoulder. He turned him, placing himself on Noah's left, between him and the table.

"Out ye go, ye sneak! I'll talk to ye outside—and maybe see your employer sacks ye, to boot. Gentlemen," he requested the others, "pray resume. Leave this miscreant to me. I've had some experience dealing with unprincipled scoundrels!"

They took another step together, and another, and a third. The door lay around one end of the oval table, and Noah, keeping his face averted from the group, had the space measured in inches. Once outside without Angus MacAuliffe recognizing him—

But it was not to be. The planter's crackling tones made his heartbeat falter.

"Hold on, sir!" MacAuliffe in two strides came around the table-end. He stared piercingly at Noah. At first there was nothing positive in his look; but then anger gave a dangerous sheen to his slate-hued eyes. His breath came faster and his thick fists clenched.

"So!" he ejaculated. "'Tis you, eh? Scoundrelly assassin that ye are, ye thought to elude me? Why—" With an effort MacAuliffe checked imprecations ready to his lips. He turned.

"Gentlemen, your waiter is none other than a bound-boy lately fled my plantation. A dastardly young rascal, 'pon my word! In his impudence a month since he tripped me and caused a horse to crack my skull with its hoofs! I'll—"

"Just a moment, Mr. MacAuliffe," Mr. Jones interrupted coolly. "Are ye not exaggerating? I well recall that day. Your—er, health was not of the best, sir. Ye were quite unsteady on your feet—"

Noah became aware of something prodding, prodding him in the small of the back. Instinctively he reached back there and almost started at the feel of a hard object well-shaped to his hand being offered him.

It was a pistol.

MacAuliffe's face grew redder at Mr. Jones's effrontery and one of his storms of temper was fast clouding his fleshy face.

"Hold on, sir!" he roared. "I'll have no jay bird from Tobago instruct me on my health! Nor keep me from a low-lived, rascally—"

Noah sprang to get his back to the wall. Facing MacAuliffe, he brought the pistol to aim at the planter's chest.

There was silence. MacAuliffe's eyes played unbelievingly on the weapon. They wrenched to Noah's face. And what he read there held him silent another instant.

"Come, come!" exclaimed Mr. Jefferson. "You really shouldn't—"

"Put the weapon down!" commanded Mr. Hewes angrily.

"He is a spy, then!" Doctor Read waved a fist at Noah. "You traitorous Tory! You overheard every detail, every—"

"Gentlemen, please don't move." Noah as from

afar heard his own voice in level tones defying the group. "Mr. MacAuliffe, I've no intention of giving myself up to your cruelty, whatever the cost. I trust," he added, commencing to glory in command of his enemy, "you completely understand me?"

As he spoke he sidled toward the door. An anxious question twisted and turned in his brain: was it locked? For a glance had shown there was no key on this side. Meanwhile he held them all at bay, but his weapon was pointed at Mr. MacAuliffe. And, verily, Noah thought, he would squeeze the trigger if the planter made the least movement to seize him.

MacAuliffe read his danger in the black muzzle of the gun and in the glittering eyes of his escaped bound-boy. His face took on a purplish tinge, as if he were about to suffer a stroke. But he did not move and his wrath was so great that he could only puff incoherently.

Noah grasped the doorknob behind him. It turned readily and the door yielded! A last instant he faced the conferees.

"Sirs, I have no Loyalist sympathy in my body. I am a Patriot as much as any of you. In time to come I mean to prove that. But I am indentured to Mr. MacAuliffe and have no intention of returning to his evil brand of slavery. Gentlemen—good night!"

In a flash he was outside, slamming the door. The

key was there and he twisted it just as Angus MacAuliffe sought to yank the door wide to pursue.

Turning, Noah darted along the corridor to the rear stairs. In another moment he was crouched at their bottom, listening. One of the kitchen maids, finished with her night's work, was just leaving the inn, but she was unaware of his presence. When the outer door closed behind her, Noah stepped cat-like to it. He paused, listening to the muffled imprecations and shouts for assistance from the second-floor parlor. A wan smile stamped his face and hopefully he let himself out into the cool night, shutting the door in his wake.

For a moment he stood irresolute. To flee in either direction along the highway seemed to invite capture. Ought he to seek hiding in Fredericksburg? It was a sizable town and should offer concealment.

Eyes narrowed, he considered. He did not know Fredericksburg well. Besides, it seemed likely that Angus MacAuliffe would ransack the streets hunting him. Perhaps some obvious place would be least suspect for the time being, the safer because of its very closeness.

He stole from shadow to shadow of the inn's outbuildings. Pausing, Noah guessed from louder cries that MacAuliffe and the others had been released from the second-floor parlor. His former master would quickly organize searchers, including the sheriff and the Fredericksburg constable, without doubt.

Reaching the smaller of two barns, he entered. Carriage horses stomped and moved about in the stalls, their harness rustling. Noah saw the front door of the Virginia House open to a rectangle of light, saw MacAuliffe rush out followed by three other men.

"Search every building first! Then we'll take the highway and the town!"

"Sir, a man seeking escape wouldn't delay," someone called.

"Search, I tell ye. Search!"

Hurriedly Noah mounted the ladder to the haymow. It was inky dark there, yielding a friendliness that soothed the wild fluttering in his stomach. He made his way to a far corner where the eaves came at an acute angle so that he had to drop on his knees, then for the last few feet, crawl. He stretched full-length alongside the eaves, able to hear everything in the courtyard and covered with hay against an inspection of the mow.

Worried lest he had not chosen wisely, he lay listening. Whoever the men were who were helping MacAuliffe's search, they were not the gentlemen of the secret conference. Probably they were the sheriff or his deputies or the town constable, for Noah had marked how such men liked loitering in the Virginia House taproom rather than faithfully making their rounds. Now and again, emerging from buildings or behind them, they called out their lack of success.

"Scour the highway for ten miles each way—that's what we ought to be doing!" one growled to another.

"It's either there or crouchin' in a Fredericksburg shed ye'll find the rascal," his comrade agreed.

Noah tensed as he heard someone enter the barn below him. Through floor cracks he could see gleams of yellow light from a lantern moving in and out of the stalls. The haymow would be inspected next . . . Had he selected well? For there was no dodging now. He was trapped if discovered where he lay.

Of course, he had the pistol. In some surprise he found himself still gripping it in his right fist. But he knew he would not shoot anyone. To do so would but make his seeming guilt the greater.

Lantern rays danced higher on the slanted inside roof as a man climbed the ladder to the mow. Scarcely breathing, Noah crouched lower, waiting and watching the rays through the hay that covered him.

The searcher stomped about, raising his lantern to see into every corner, dissipate every shadow. Once he stood within eight feet and it seemed an hour the man remained, though it was but seconds.

Grunting, the fellow returned to the ladder and the yellow rays of light receded and were gone.

Thankfully, Noah released his held breath. He lay listening to shouts that became talk as half a dozen men gathered in the courtyard, MacAuliffe among them.

"Sure ye covered everything?" he demanded in disappointment.

"He isn't about, sir."

"No, he wouldn't be. Fleeing, that's what he's been doin' while we waste time!" growled another.

"Well,—" Angus MacAuliffe seemed reluctant to leave—"we'll get our horses then and go by twos up and down the highway and through the town. That's where he'll likely be found," he decided grimly. "And mind, when ye do nab him, careful of his pistol. For he's a rascal and desperate, and he may use it."

Another few minutes saw them mounted. There were final instructions; then the rattle of horses' hoofs floated to Noah, and the searchers went their ways.

Moving to a more comfortable position, he lay resting a while, thinking. How long must he hide here? Until two or three days elapsed? But that was not good to think of because of the inaction of it. And there was the matter of food. Mr. Frenewell, the proprietor of the Virginia House, doubtless now

Scarcely Breathing, Noah Crouched Lower

thought Noah the rascal Angus MacAuliffe claimed him to be. Even if the host had no such belief, a man serving the public as he did could ill afford to aid someone sought by the law.

He wanted to leave here, quickly, and to put miles between himself and Fredericksburg—many miles. But there was the risk of being caught as he went.

Crawling to a knothole, Noah found the courtyard below empty. He located Eileen's room and saw that it was dark, doubtless indicating she was abed. Perhaps she knew nothing of the chase. Then, as he stared at the inn, he saw the golden light vanish in the second-floor parlor, indicating that the conference had ended. The men soon would emerge, mount their horses and carriages, and disperse.

For a moment he pondered his plan. Making his way to the ladder, Noah began to climb down it. Perhaps he was careless, for suddenly, his hold failing, he tumbled the last five feet and went sprawling on the floor. Captain Jones's pistol, which he had held in one hand, knocked on a step of the ladder, then on planking beside his head.

Unhurt, he picked himself up. He was thankful the pistol had not discharged since its report might have betrayed him. Fumbling, he located it, and noticed at once that the hammer was down. It had been cocked when he aimed the weapon at Mr.

MacAuliffe, and Noah had not known how to uncock it. Now the hammer was down. Yet the weapon had not exploded . . .

He stood frowning a moment before he understood. His frown gave way to wonder. Noah felt carefully of the pistol, and what his fingers reported verified his suspicion, made him chuckle.

"If Mr. MacAuliffe could but know! All he needed to do there in the parlor was seize me and I'd have been his bound-boy once more. The pistol wasn't loaded!"

Suddenly he realized that Mr. John Paul Jones had known this. He would not want his weapon used to wound and possibly kill any gentleman in the evening's conference. At the same time, having little stomach for MacAuliffe, he had desired to aid Noah. And he had, effectively enough!

CHAPTER EIGHT

WITH MR. HENRY

Still smiling in the dark about his unloaded pistol, Noah waited. One of the Negro stablemen came with a lantern, selected a horse, and led him outside. After a bit he came for another, and another. This continued for twenty minutes, but each time the man selected horses other than those Noah waited for.

At last he watched the pair of matched bays led forth. Noah went outside and around the rear corner of the barn to stand in its shadow. The horses were hitched to a covered buggy and the stableman waited at their heads while men drifted, talking, from the Virginia House.

"Ready?" floated the voice Noah waited to hear. The tall, slender man handed money to the stableman and got into the carriage. He took the reins, adjusted them, and spoke to the horses. They moved toward the highway at a walk.

Noah darted back to the rear of the barn, climbed a fence, crossed another small yard and another fence. Panting, he crouched beside willows fringing the highway. When the carriage had just passed he ran out, gripped a wide rear spring, and jumped to a seated posture on the rear axle. He was none too soon for the horses broke into a trot at once.

It was not a comfortable seat he had, bouncing along on the axle, for the highway was badly rutted from spring rains. Yet Noah was not thinking of that but of whether he was noticeable. Deciding he was, he turned sideways, bent his knees, and crouched against the overhanging body of the carriage.

Now he was all right. Mr. Patrick Henry, whose carriage it was, did not intend passing through Fredericksburg, he knew from a remark Mr. Henry had made during the meeting. His home lay some eight miles beyond the town, so he would take the shorter road at the fork they must be approaching now.

Sounds of voices startled Noah:

"—too bad your horse went lame, Doctor Read. However, Frenewell's stableman will care for him."

"Yes. I'll send someone to fetch him in a day or two. I'm under obligation to you, Mr. Henry, for this lift."

" 'Tis nothing, sir. I shall be glad to take you to your door in town."

Noah swallowed hard. Instead of going the safe country route, he was being taken the dangerous way!

He saw the fork slip past and knew Mr. Henry had selected the main street of Fredericksburg. For an instant he was impelled to jump from his perch and hurry back to the barn of the Virginia House. For there might be searchers abroad in Fredericksburg who would collar him.

He resolved to risk detection. Shrinking himself harder against the coach, he peered this way and that along the darkened streets as they moved deeper into the town. Something like panic seized him as the horses fell to a walk and the equipage veered to a sidewalk.

The sway and creaking proved Doctor Read getting out. "My thanks to you, Mr. Henry. And we shall be seeing each other again. Good night!"

"Good night, Doctor." The horses started up, then halted as a new voice rang out.

"Sorry, sir." A man with a lantern flashed it inside the carriage. "We're on the watch for that bound-boy of Mr. MacAuliffe's, and I only wanted to make sure who was in the carriage."

"Then you haven't got him yet? I haven't seen him, myself."

"We'll nab him, all right. I needn't detain you, Mr. Henry." Then he added, "Perhaps I'll just take a look in case he's riding with you and you don't know it."

Swiftly Noah jumped from his perch. Watching the yellow lantern rays, he crept away from them around the side of the carriage. His heart thudded with alarm and any instant he expected the watchman to glimpse his legs through the wheels.

But the man took only a cursory glance without leaving the sidewalk. As Mr. Henry spoke to the horses, Noah trotted beside the carriage. They went thus for more than half a square; then, the watchman having been left behind, Noah dropped back, seized the heavy spring, and swung himself onto the axle once more.

With vast relief he watched Fredericksburg disappear. The carriage gained open country and rolled along for a mile or more. Then it slowed and finally came to a stop. In renewed apprehension he heard Mr. Henry dismounting.

Noah stood in the road. The dark figure of Mr. Henry came alongside the rear wheel. Each could see the other now, and for an instant neither spoke.

"Are you the boy who served our meeting?"

"Yes, sir," Noah said with difficulty.

"Hmm. Thought I felt some weight back here. Usually this carriage rides very lightly." He paused. "You are the bound-boy Mr. MacAuliffe desires to retake?"

"Yes, sir." Noah swallowed, seeking a note of confidence in his voice. "I—I don't want to go back. Are you going to—hand me over to him?"

He thought a moment. "At any rate, lad, you may as well ride more comfortably. Come up with me."

Noah knew he could dart away from Mr. Henry and escape. Certainly he could outrun the older man, and he doubted Mr. Henry would even attempt pursuit. But something made him walk past him and climb silently into the carriage. In a moment the other sat beside him and was clucking the horses to a trot.

"You had a very unceremonious method of entering our meeting—spilling through that skylight," Mr. Henry remarked dryly.

"I'm sorry, sir. I slipped somehow and just tumbled in. I was trying to get away from Mr. MacAuliffe—" Noah stopped, wondering whether he should speak freely.

"Oh? Had he known you were about?"

"He suspected only. I fled his plantation a month since. Of course I should have gone farther away. But Mr. Frenewell treated me well and I wished to earn money and I have no plans," Noah said. "Then to my consternation Mr. MacAuliffe and his niece arrived. He didn't recognize me in the dark, but I had to carry the lady's trunk to her room.

"Presently—" he sighed, "—I was hiding in the trunk. When Mr. MacAuliffe stepped out, I left by the window. 'Twas while I was creeping down the roof that I looked in on your meeting. But honestly, I had no intention of spying, Mr. Henry."

"I'm relieved to hear that. A moment ago you

"You May as Well Ride Comfortably."

used the word 'consternation.' Have you had schooling?"

"My mother taught me, sir, when we lived in Trinidad, then in Norfolk. I was studying geometry and Greek when she died. Before I found myself indentured."

"You 'found' yourself indentured?"

"My mother was a lady, sir. I don't understand why she indentured me. It happened just before she died. My father is long dead," Noah added. He disliked being questioned about his father, about whom he knew so little.

"So then you lived with Mr. MacAuliffe?"

"Not exactly. With the slaves."

Mr. Henry glanced at him in surprise. They drove a way without speaking.

"Well, lad? Have you nothing to say about Mr. MacAuliffe?"

"I tried my best to please him, Mr. Henry, but I could not. Indeed, no one could. At last, when he was scolding me about a plow horse much too ill to be worked, Mr. MacAuliffe was unsteady from liquor and got himself kicked. He blamed me, though 'twas not in the least my doing. Later, after I'd got him home, he came at me with his sword and— Well, I snatched it away and broke it. So then he vowed to have me flogged, and I ran away."

"Well," reflected Mr. Henry, "if I were a fugitive

bound-boy, I should tell some such story. It gains sympathy, whether true or not. You see what I mean? Your name is—"

"Noah Carr, sir. Yes, I see what you mean. You cannot know if I speak the truth. And though there are those who would verify me, I am in no circumstances to reach them and ask them to do it."

The carriage rolled along in the night. Mr. Henry shifted his position.

"Mr. MacAuliffe seems one of our ardent Patriots. His knowledge gained in serving with the Royal Navy may be of use to us."

"I didn't know Mr. MacAuliffe had been in the Navy, sir. Nor had I known he was a Patriot. That is," Noah amended, "I never heard him say he was a Patriot. It surprised me to find him in your meeting." He added, "I believe Mr. John Paul Jones might vouch for me, sir, if he chose to. He was present at the beginning of the incident but had gone when the horse kicked Mr. MacAuliffe. And he recognized me while I served you gentlemen tonight."

Mr. Henry watched the flanks of his horses several minutes.

Noah asked, "Sir, is there to be a Continental Navy? And will Mr. Jones serve in it?"

His companion glanced at him in the dark. "The Congress must decide both matters, as they will in due time. You know," he pursued, "I am a law-abiding citizen and—"

"Excuse me, Mr. Henry. Did I not hear with my own ears that you intend rebelling against the King? And I, sir, am also rebelling against oppression. Though, like you, in all other things I am law-abiding."

Mr. Henry coughed, though it sounded suspiciously like a chuckle. "Nevertheless I deem it my duty to hand over to the law any escaping slave or indentured servant I may apprehend."

Noah had a sinking feeling. "Yes, sir."

"Of course," Mr. Henry mused, "if a fugitive threatened me with a weapon and forced me to give him a ride for a distance, perhaps I should be unable to capture him. Let us say he captured me—with a pistol. Then I couldn't hand him over to the law, I suppose."

Noah sat forward with excited relief. "No, sir! And—" He fumbled in his belt. "Here's the pistol, Mr. Henry! Now you will hand me over to the law at your own peril, sir!"

He thought his host was chuckling, but again it turned to a cough. "Then I'm at your mercy," Mr. Henry sighed. "Tell me, Noah—now you have the upper hand—where are you going and what do you intend doing?"

"I'm going far away, sir. At least to Richmond,

and perhaps out of Virginia. Yes, that should be safer. And I asked about the Continental Navy because if Mr. Jones will command a ship, I wish to be with him."

"You do? You want to be a seaman?"

"Yes, sir. At least, I want to fight Redcoats. I am heart and soul with the colonies and mean to do my part. And from what I heard tonight, it seems perhaps Mr. Jones will be commanding a ship. By my faith," Noah exclaimed, "I hope he'll have me!"

He checked his enthusiasm as the carriage turned off the highway and up a winding road to a mansion set well back among tall trees. As if feeling Noah's questioning eyes on him, Mr. Henry nodded.

"This is my home, called 'Scotchtown.' I've a fine family of six children, and there's plenty of space for 'em to grow up in. Noah," he jested, "do you intend robbing me of my horses and carriage? Remember, I've only carried you because you forced it at pistol-point."

"Oh, no, sir. Mr. Henry, can you help me get in the navy?"

"No, since there's no navy as yet. But if you get to Philadelphia you might chance to see Mr. Joseph Hewes, or perhaps Mr. Jones. You could put your question to either gentleman."

He stopped the carriage. "One question, and please answer it carefully. Do you consider Mr.

MacAuliffe a staunch Patriot?"

Noah hesitated. "Sir, he did not confide his political sentiments to me. But I am unable to think him a Patriot.

"I'd best be gone before your servants come out," he added. "I'm in your debt for the ride, Mr. Henry." He climbed out. "And you've not been in much danger from the pistol," he assured.

"Enough so I daren't hand you over to the law. Yet not enough to frighten me." He climbed out the other side of the carriage. "I spied Mr. Jones giving it to you there in our meeting room but he laid my apprehension with a wink that told me the weapon was empty. It made me see that Mr. Jones felt you may have adequate grievance against your late master.

"Good night, Noah. Fight hard for liberty!" he called as a Negro came running around the corner of the house to take the horses.

In the days that followed Noah worked at many an odd job to earn a meal or the right to sleep in a haymow. Accustomed to the hard labor of the MacAuliffe plantation, he found it not too wearing to hew down a tree, split firewood, draw water, or take brief service as a stable hand for enough food to quiet the gnawing in his middle. He was young and strong and willing, and the farmers along his way were glad enough for his help.

True, many a suspicious look was accorded the tall, gangling boy who seemed to belong to no one. Sometimes, asked his home, he replied, "I hope to learn that in Philadelphia." One farmer, a man with stern gray eyes made fiercer by canopies of bushy brows, demanded to know whence Noah had fled.

It took him by surprise, and he straightened from his woodchopping. "Fled? Have I a fugitive look, would you say?"

"Ye resemble somewhat a bound-boy a gentleman came by here seeking only last week. Except maybe you're taller, most a man grown save for your skinniness. But ye could be him," the farmer growled.

Disturbed, Noah managed a careless laugh. "You could, perhaps, win a reward, sir, by handing me over to the sheriff. On the other hand, if I'm not he who is sought, I could exact a penalty for the shame of false arrest." Turning his back, he resumed swinging his ax.

The man did not give him over to the sheriff but Noah quickly departed that evening. The incident proved to him that he still was not far enough from Angus MacAuliffe for real safety.

Many good folk, however, treated him kindly and forebore asking questions. The women in particular, he found, were little concerned whether he had fled indenture but were more interested in providing food which might put meat on his bones. He learned to seek out not a farmer, but his wife, offering to do any household chore her husband misliked and skimped. His willingness and boyish good cheer usually won their hearts. With motherly solicitude they fed him and gave him facilities for bathing and sometimes contributed a cast-off article or two of clothing.

Thus his appearance underwent gradual change. Never fed quite as much as hunger demanded on the acres of Angus MacAuliffe, he found himself adding a little flesh. He was hard-muscled and tanned from the outdoor life. There was a spring in his step, a glint of self-reliance in his brown eyes, little worry in his heart about the future and lessening apprehension about the past.

His costume too was altering. The yellow weskit supplied by Calvin Frenewell of the Virginia House got itself badly torn on a fence and had to be discarded. One of the bronze shoe buckles was lost along some highway. His coat became dusty and worn, patched with lighter blue by a good-hearted housewife, and later patched again in brown until Frenewell would never have known his garment. Noah's dark hair grew until it was brushing his shoulders. At last he carpentered a stoop for a town barber and got a bath and his head shaved in payment.

When he saw himself in the glass after this operation, he was at first startled. Then he had to laugh.

"I'm not the same man who came in here," he told the barber.

"That you are not. But you're no man or there'd be more than fuzz on your chin. You're but a boy. Tell me, have ye no home?"

Noah waved his arm in a wide half-circle. "Yes, and there 'tis. The world is my home. Good-bye to you, sir," he added, and walked jauntily out of the place.

There was talk everywhere of the impending struggle between the Colonies and the forces of King George the Third. Noah listened, wanting to learn as much about it as possible. He knew that dark hours were nearing for the Colonies and it would be many a month before either freedom or worse slavery to royal tyranny could be settled.

Folk held all varieties of views. Some disapproved resistance against the edicts of Parliament. Though they might agree that the Quartering Act, forcing colonial householders to lodge soldiers, was unfair, yet they feared to try balking it. " 'Tis the King's will," they pointed out timidly. "What can we do?" In the minds of these, traditional respect for the King's laws was too great to be violated. And the power of His Majesty's army and navy overawed them.

"If we owe obedience to the King, does not he owe us justice?" another group argued. Some thought George the Third unaware of the tyrannous rule of his officials. "We'll make a stir of resistance," they proposed. "It will come to His Majesty's attention, then he'll right our wrongs."

The vigorous Patriots sneered at this. "We've made many a stir—and to what gain? Did the Boston Tea Party prove to His Majesty there's wrong in the tea tax? And did he lessen it? Instead we gained the Coercive Acts, making our lot worse. Every resistance has brought on our heads not justice," they argued, "but oppression in worse form."

Many persons felt that far-off Massachusetts must be tenanted by hotheads, since most outbreaks against authority happened there. Others pointed out: " 'Tis because the Bay Colony is seafaring. There is much shipping out and importing, and unfair laws have taken all rights of importation away from America. Thus Massachusetts suffers more gravely than we do, who are only in small part seafaring."

"Then let Massachusetts fight her battles!" retorted others. "If the need comes, we shall fight ours."

"No, no," protested men who felt that all colonies were affected. "How can Massachusetts fight the King's soldiers? All thirteen colonies must band together, else all battles are lost before they are started."

So it went, with every shade of opinion. Even the more intelligent slaves supported one side or the other. It was known everywhere that in the Boston Massacre a Negro named Crispus Attucks had been slain, and this made some slaves declare he should have been at home doing his master's work, and others say perhaps the day of freedom was near.

Among small farmers Noah found the issues often ill-understood. Many did not realize that heavy taxes caused the high prices of their imported teas, spices, sugar, tools, and other articles. A few had found they must pay taxes to the King two thousand miles away when they bought or sold land. Some had been in jail in England for petty crimes and so had developed a hate for the King's authority which, when they came to America, thrust them on the Patriots' side. Others, busy tilling their land and raising families, were not interested in the controversy.

"Let the rich merchants and the big landowners fight if they want. We'll plow our fields in peace," was their view.

Weighing this argument and that, seeking to learn the truth of the matter, Noah worked and traveled and listened and pondered. He could not but believe that, as Poor Richard said: *Where there is smoke there must be fire.* Honest folk were unlikely to risk their property and even their necks without grave reason. Though he had precious little money himself, he realized that trade was stifled by taxes too heavy to bear. He knew that men engaged in shipping saw all profitable business withheld by law for the East India Company—and it was known that the Company had got laws passed solely to enrich itself. Noah could understand, too, the anger of colonists such as those in New York especially, at being forced to lodge soldiers in their own parlors and bedrooms.

News was slow-spreading and not always reliable. However, it was really war now. General Gage had sailed into Boston harbor, landed his troops, and occupied the city. Boston was under martial law. Trade there was at a standstill. Suffering was rife from lack of employment, lack of provisions and of clothing.

General George Washington had drilled his volunteers as best he could without proper equipment, and he was besieging Boston. How this would turn out, none could say. Some Virginian Loyalists called General Washington a traitor, since as a young man he had served the King on surveying missions into western lands. Others said he should not mix with the affairs of Massachusetts, for New Englanders always were disgruntled about something. Others, like Patrick Henry and Richard Henry Lee, declared Washington to be a great Patriot and prophesied that he would chase General Gage and his Redcoats into the sea.

The Continental Congress was sitting in Philadelphia. Noah, working from town to town, farm to farm, determined to go there. He wanted to see the Congress in session, if possible. Too, he hoped to learn whether there was to be a navy, and if so, whether Mr. Jones would take him as a sailor.

CHAPTER NINE

IN PHILADELPHIA

On a warm July morning Noah found himself walking along Broad Street in Philadelphia. He had slept in a livery barn on the outskirts of the city, awakened at dawn, and washed himself carefully in a trough of water intended for horses. Extra care over the past two weeks had kept his costume reasonably clean, for he did not want to look like a country lout as he strolled through the great city.

Nor did he present an ill appearance, Noah thought with some pride. His thigh-length coat of dark blue broadcloth he had bought with labor from a widow whose husband had owned it. And it was well-made and not too worn, though slack from his shoulders because tailored for a heavier man. His tan whipcord breeches were serviceable. He had no weskit but his gray homespun shirt was plain and good. His shoes were good—at any rate to Noah. He had paid out most of his money for them and they were durable and had large iron buckles.

Broad Street, he thought, must be an important street in Philadelphia. It was cobbled and had narrow sidewalks and there was scarce a vacant lot. Red brick homes stood one against the other. On corners there usually were stores. At this morning hour the street was just coming to life, with an occasional heavy dray passing, a merchant flinging back shutters, a housemaid scrubbing the front step.

Noah smiled as he remembered that Doctor Benjamin Franklin's first day in Philadelphia must have been something like this. He had arrived here a boy and was said to have trudged about the city with a penny loaf of bread under one arm, wondering where to start at seeking his fortune. It was also said that young Ben Franklin had fallen in love at sight of a pretty young girl scrubbing her father's doorstep, and that years later he married her. But Noah, glancing at the buxom maids scrubbing here and there, felt no prick of Cupid's arrows. He was conscious only of hunger.

He turned down a side street, seeking a bakery. Presently like young Franklin years before, he had bought a long loaf of French bread for a penny and was strolling along munching it.

"I wonder where Doctor Franklin lives," he reflected. "I should like to see him. Perhaps he would just be coming out."

He inquired, but without result until he asked a constable. The man looked him up and down. "And is the Doctor expecting you?" he inquired.

"No," Noah admitted, biting off a mouthful of bread. He had to chew a moment before he could speak more. "He is a great man and I pray to catch a glimpse of him. Have you ever read 'Poor Richard,' sir?"

"Gad, boy, I can't read. But I know the sayings well. 'Penny wise and pound foolish.' 'Half a loaf is better than none,' " he quoted. "Is that you?"

They both laughed as Noah instinctively looked at his loaf. The constable leaned against a building, a friendly fellow. "I see you're but fresh from the country. Are the crops goin' to be good this year?"

Chagrined, Noah looked himself over.

" 'Tis the dust on your shoes," the other explained. "And a bit of hay clingin' to your cap. But I asked," he went on, "because with all the folk come to this city for jawin' about politics, I wonder if anyone's left on the farms?"

"Jawin'? You mean the Congress?"

"I mean nothin' else. Jawin', jawin' all day long. When will they get to business? Though I hear somethin' secret they're brewin' will be like twistin' the British lion's tail. Likely it'll make him roar—with cannon," the officer said darkly.

"I don't understand," Noah frowned.

"Nor I, exactly. But the Congress is— Well," he said cautiously, "ask Doctor Franklin. He's a ringleader, he is. Mr. Thomas Jefferson's another, and Mr. John Adams another.

"But I must be off." He straightened and brushed

his shoulder. "If ye want to see where a great and fine man lives, go two blocks down, then one to the right. You can tell the house because it has that lightning rod on't."

"A lightning rod?"

"It's one of Doctor Franklin's inventions. He's toyed with—uh, electricity, I think it's called. You know, the flashin' light out of the sky in a storm? Doctor Franklin fastened up a long metal rod on his house, and he says it'll never be struck. The lightning will travel down the rod into the ground without harm. You'll see it stickin' up from the roof—quite a newfangled thing. But if ye ask me," he ended, "when the Lord sends down a bolt, ye can't escape what's to be. Well, pleasant day."

Noah strolled on. Following the directions, he did find a narrow, three-story red brick dwelling with a queer metal rod thrusting up from its roof. He crossed to sit on the curb in front of the place, his feet in the gutter. Munching his bread, he waited.

A Negro woman came out to scrub the step. "Is your owner, Doctor Franklin, at home?" Noah called.

She leaned on her broom, regarding him. "Doct' Franklin ain't got no slave. I ain't got no owner. He don't hold no truck with slave'y!"

"Oh. Well, is he likely to appear soon?"

She shook her head. "He writin' in his study since dawn. He so busy, dat man eat with one hand and write with de othah. He jus' come and go and work and work." She resumed her scrubbing.

Noah waited an hour. About to wander off, he heard a door open and voices. Turning, he saw a rather plump man, plainly dressed, coming out of the house. The Negro woman called after him and fetched the three-cornered hat he had forgotten. As the plump man descended to the sidewalk carrying papers rolled under his arm, Noah saw that he was indeed elderly. He walked with a slight limp, as if afflicted with rheumatism, and his face was lined and he wore strange half-lensed spectacles.

This was all the impression he got before the gentleman, seeing him in the street, called a cheery, "Good morning, young man. Why aren't you at work?"

"Good morning, Doctor Franklin." He had to collect his wits. "I've just come to Philadelphia, sir. I wanted to see you."

"Me?" Doctor Franklin leaned on his black cane. "What about?"

"Nothing, sir. I wanted to see the man who wrote about Poor Richard, sir. And invented lightning rods."

"Hmm. Well, as Poor Richard would say, 'Waste not and want not.' There's more writing to be done

"Good Morning, Dr. Franklin," Said Noah

and there are oceans of useful things to be invented. Like stoves. Contrive one'll throw off more heat. I've invented a good one," he informed Noah, "but it may be you could improve it. There's nothing in the world that can't be made better.

"Here." He felt in his weskit, took out a penny, and tossed it to Noah. "Always carry that. It'll remind you to be industrious. If you are, and have good sense, you'll make your fortune. You may think the penny is a good-luck piece but it'll be your industry'll be the lucky thing. Good-bye."

"Good-bye, Doctor Franklin. Thank you, sir."

He stood watching him limp rapidly away. At every doorstep where someone spoke to him he gave a cheery reply and a wave of his cane. His progress left a street sprinkled with smiles, until he turned the corner and was gone.

Noah felt awed. Doctor Franklin had taken time to speak to him—nay, more, to give him a lucky piece! He stared at the coin and tossed and caught it. Then he put it in his pocket. His impulse was to follow Doctor Franklin; but he decided it would not be seemly.

Chewing the last of the loaf, he resumed his wandering. He thought proudly of the several important men he had met and how they all had treated him well. There were Doctor Franklin, Mr. Jefferson, Mr. Joseph Hewes, and Mr. Henry and others. The distinguished gentlemen had, in fact, treated him better than had many a lesser man. It was something to puzzle over.

"Perhaps, as Poor Richard says," he mused, " 'The busy man has time for everything.' And that includes courtesy to all."

The size and complexity of Philadelphia continued to fascinate him as he strolled here and there, staring at all the sights. Resting awhile in the main square, he saw gentlemen entering and leaving the State House, a gracefully spired red brick building facing one side of the park. There, he knew, the Continental Congress had been sitting since May.

Noah rose and sauntered over to the entrance, but found admission denied him. An important secret session was in progress, said the officer at the door, and visitors were not permitted. Disappointed, Noah returned to the lawn, sitting with his back to a tree and watching life ebb and flow around him.

It was to see Philadelphia and speak to Mr. John Paul Jones that he had come here. Now he had accomplished some of the first, what about the second? But he scarcely knew where to start seeking Mr. Jones. Perhaps he would be staying at some inn, perhaps with friends, perhaps in a rented room.

Rested from his walking, Noah decided to ask at inns near the square. But no one seemed to have heard of that particular Mr. Jones. Discouraged, he stood on a street corner, thinking. Turning on his heel, he entered the last inn he had visited and inquired:

"Can you tell me where I may find Mr. Joseph Hewes?"

"Mr. Hewes? You mean of North Carolina?"

"Yes, that is he. Is he here?"

"He lives here, yes. But he's attending the Congress." The haughty clerk looked Noah up and down. "He's a very busy man and has no time to waste on loafers."

"Sir," Noah retorted, "if I judged you as hastily as you judge me, your face'd turn red as King George's coat. Good day!"

He marched out. At any rate he had learned where Mr. Hewes resided, and thought he would wait. But he had sat on the curbstone only half an hour when his eyes widened and he sprang to his feet. Heedless of approaching horses, Noah darted to the opposite walk. He halted, panting.

"Mr. Jones! If you please, sir!"

The short, strong-shouldered man in black who had emerged from the tavern turned around. He frowned as if puzzled. Then remembrance came in his pale blue eyes.

"Ah!" He knew Noah now. "Young man, you do seem to dog my steps. Have you come to return my—" He glanced around. "The article I lent you?"

"Well, no, sir. Not exactly. The fact is, I—I don't have it any more."

Mr. Jones looked serious. "No? Such articles have a certain value, er—"

"Noah Carr, sir. I'm sorry I don't have the pistol, but I feared to continue carrying it. Should I be questioned and perhaps searched, it might have made my situation worse to be armed. And even though 'twas empty, folk might still think me armed," Noah explained.

"I see what you mean. Still, hadn't you a certain responsibility to return a borrowed item?"

Noah's eyes fell. "Yes, sir. I left it with Mr. Patrick Henry. He gave me a ride, and I tucked it behind the cushion in his carriage. I'll try to make it up to you sometime, Mr. Jones," he promised.

"I'll depend on that. You are to make up my loss when occasion makes that possible. But, Noah," he continued curiously, "what do you want of me?"

"I want to serve under you in the Continental Navy, sir," he said promptly.

Mr. Jones started to smile but left off. He examined Noah from head to foot. "Aren't you aware that there is no navy? That's why I'm not in it, because it doesn't exist. Besides, are you a sailor?"

"No, sir. I know nothing about ships. But I can

learn. I expect you once did, Mr. Jones," he pointed out respectfully.

"Well, yes, that's true. However, when I was your age I knew quite a lot about vessels, having sailed since I was fourteen." He thought a moment, then moved closer to the tavern wall, beckoning Noah to follow. "I shan't ask about your past. I don't wish to know much about it. Are you sure," he inquired seriously, "that you want to be a sailor? That you're ready to fight and perhaps be killed?"

"It was in the hope of serving under you, sir, that I came to Philadelphia. And since we're at war, I intend to do my part."

Mr. Jones eyed him steadily. "Why not join General Washington's army up in Massachusetts?"

"I prefer to be in the navy. Will there be one, Mr. Jones?"

He gestured hopelessly. "I've stayed here, rotting on my keel, trying to get the answer you also want. But Congress has been immersed in a thousand other matters deemed to be more important. A Naval Committee has been formed and has accomplished nothing. Nothing!" he repeated bitterly.

There was silence. "Well, sir, do you expect there will be a navy some time?"

"Oh, yes. About the time the British fleet's blockade of our coast has starved us into submission. After the war, say." He shook his head. "Mr. Hewes is trying his best, and a few other gentlemen, but there is no result as yet. I've offered my services, Noah, and they are ignored. What is a sailor without a ship?"

Noah kicked disappointedly at the sidewalk. "I'd planned on serving with you, sir. I thought perhaps I'd be of some use."

"You'd be of more use with a voyage or two in your past. Look," Mr. Jones proposed, laying a hand on his shoulder, "if you are determined—and I think you are—why not go to sea? Though I am half frantic with idleness, Mr. Hewes gives me reason to hope a navy will some day be formed. We shall need hands then, experienced and willing hands. Landlubbers are but dead weight when there's a gale tearing your sails. Then you need seamen!"

Noah blinked. "I expect I'll hear of it when you are given a vessel," he reflected. "Will it be in this port, can you guess?"

"It might be any port—here, New York, even Boston if General Washington throws the Redcoats out."

"Then I may hope to join you, sir, when the time comes?"

Mr. Jones's smile had an ingratiating quality no one could resist. "I shall be needing alert hands if ever I get a ship. You might ask me then. But, mind, I'll have no use for seasick landlubbers. Where are you bound for now?" he added.

Noah stood straighter. "Which direction is't to the port?"

"Down that street yonder. Why?"

Noah moved away. "I'll start at once, then. I mean to ship on the handiest vessel and start learning what I must know to cease being a landlubber."

Mr. Jones's chuckle floated after him. "Good! Sign on a brigantine if you can!"

CHAPTER TEN

IN THE AMERICAN NAVY

It was clear but biting cold that morning of January 14, 1776. Despite the braziers with their glowing red coals, the chill penetrated between decks of the *Alfred* where Seaman Noah Carr sat with his back against a bulkhead, splicing a rope and listening to the talk of half a dozen of his shipmates.

At the shrill piping of the bos'n's whistle the men dropped whatever they were doing and hurried for the main deck. Noah followed, pulling on his blue-striped stocking cap. As he took his place in the ranks forming abaft the mainmast under the stern eyes of Second Lieutenant Olney he saw the shore thronged with citizens of Philadelphia to the very edges of the wharves. On the seven vessels anchored near by that with the *Alfred* comprised the new fleet, the crews were scrambling to vantage points in the rigging.

Forward on the *Alfred* Captain Dudley Saltonstall, just arrived from Boston to take command, stood with First Lieutenant John Paul Jones. In blue dress uniforms and cockade hats they waited near the gangway, watching the barge sent to the foot of Walnut Street return bearing Commander-in-

Chief Esek Hopkins.

"Seamen Boyce and Carr!" called Lieutenant Olney. The two promptly stepped forward. "To the mainmast halyards, Boyce. Carr, fetch the flag!"

The men saluted. Noah hurried below to the flag-locker, secured the folded silk pennant, and returned to stand holding it with outstretched arms at the mainmast. The bugle sounded as Commander Hopkins came aboard while the crew stood stiffly at attention. He advanced to a spot near the mainmast.

"You may proceed, Captain Saltonstall."

Captain Saltonstall turned. "Proceed, Lieutenant Jones."

At a word from the Lieutenant, Boyce prepared the halyards. Quickly he and Noah fastened on the flag. The crew remained at attention, every eye on Lieutenant Jones as he pulled in the hoisting-line hand over hand.

The flag jerking higher fell open, of vivid yellow silk with a dark-embroidered rattlesnake on it and the motto: *Don't Tread on Me*. When it was clewed at the mast-tip high above the deck, Lieutenant Olney smilingly nodded.

The men burst into cheers. Officers and men waved their caps, and cheers and waving came from the dark figures clinging to the ratlines and shrouds of the seven sister vessels, while the wharves

Every Eye Was Proudly on the Flag

of Philadelphia were a bedlam of waving and cheering at sight of the first official flag ever to fly over an American man-o'-war.

Some months later, Noah, with his pea-jacket collar turned up and his mittened hands clasping the icy rail, watched the foamy wake of the *Alfred* scudding south somewhere off New England. The long cruise raiding British shipping around Newfoundland was nearing an end. Staring over the taffrail at the cold, bouncing green waves, he thought of all that had happened since that historic day of hoisting the flag. Yes, and before that, since John Paul Jones advised him to learn to be a seaman if he wanted to fight in the American Navy when it came into being.

Well, he was no veteran seaman yet, though he'd had half a dozen voyages. Noah smiled as he pictured himself that day in Philadelphia, a country boy, studying the vessels tied up and not knowing a sloop from a brigantine or a bark.

He remembered an old salt's disgusted look when he inquired the difference. The man ceased whittling as he sat on a piling. He took the pipe out of his mouth and spat.

"Yonder's a sloop." He pointed. "One tall mast. Rigged fore-and-aft, which means one edge o' the mains'l is for'ard and t'other to the stern. Yonder's a brigantine." He pointed again. "Two masts. Square-rigged—the canvas faces for'ard.

"Now," he went on, "yonder's a barkentine coaster. See her three masts? The for'ard two are square-rigged, but the mizzen's rigged fore-and-aft. And when she wants all the wind she carries a fore-and-aft fores'l."

The *Alfred* Noah was now in was a sloop, lower in the water and a faster sailer than the other types. Barkentines and brigantines were cargo carriers, broader of beam and hence more roomy. It was on a bark that Noah had shipped for his first voyage, to Savannah and back.

Ashore after his third coasting trip, he learned that Congress had purchased several vessels and had named a list of captains and lieutenants. First on the lieutenant list was John Paul Jones, and seeking him out at an inn, Noah applied for service.

He still shivered a little at the sharp examination he had been put through. "You're no able seaman yet," Lieutenant Jones pronounced finally. "But we can use you. Mind, though, keep on learning!"

"Yes, sir," Noah promised happily.

It was difficult to sign enough experienced sailors, he knew. Several thousand seamen were serving in General Washington's army. Others sought the higher pay of crewmen on privateers—privately owned vessels which Congress permitted to arm and prey on British supply shipping. They received nearly twice Navy pay, and much more promptly. They also shared more generously in money received from the sale of ships they captured. Commander-in-Chief Hopkins, in fact, was urging Congress to halt privateering or, he said, there would never be an American Navy, for lack of men.

"How," someone grunted at Noah's elbow.

He looked up. It was Red Cherry, an Indian two or three years older who had been a sailor several years.

"How, Red Cherry. Are you on watch?"

"Me watch. We pretty soon end cruise."

"Yes, though I don't know what port we're heading to. I'll be glad for warmer weather," Noah added, tightening his collar as the keen Atlantic gale nipped frostily. "But it's been a good cruise, hasn't it, Red Cherry?"

The Indian smiled slightly. He gestured to the several other ships plowing southward with the *Alfred*. "Capture fat prizes. Take 'em home. Action plenty, but not many men killed. Captain Jones always get plenty action."

"Yes, he's made a fine record with his first command. Well, he earned the promotion. On our first cruise many of the officers were dunderheads," Noah said. "What would Commander Hopkins have captured in Abaco, down in the Bahamas, if it hadn't been for Lieutenant Jones? The Commander sailed up in broad daylight, so the Governor knew we wanted his powder supply, and shipped it out quickly. Then the Commander planned to land marines where there was no road. Why, the whole island would know they were ashore before our men got anywhere near the fort!"

"Thick in head," Red Cherry agreed. "Lieutenant Jones say take marines ashore east end of island where is road. They go. Capture hundred big guns. No man hurt. Good!"

"Yes. And later when we fought the *Glasgow* off New York. Our whole fleet against one Britisher, yet she raked us all and got away. If Lieutenant Jones had been in command, she wouldn't have! But he was below in charge of the guns."

"Court-martial fix Navy better. Throw out no-good officers." Red Cherry jerked a thumb at the short, stocky man in blue pacing the quarter-deck. "He captain now, on second cruise. We get plenty fight, burn plenty ship, capture plenty ship!"

It was against the rules to engage a man on watch in conversation lest it interfere with his vigilance. And Captain Jones, Noah had learned, was a stern disciplinarian. So he walked away from the taffrail and presently went below. Taking paper and pencil out of his locker, he settled himself in a corner of the gently heaving ship. Why not write a letter to

Eileen MacAuliffe which he could mail when he got ashore?

He had written Eileen an account of his first cruise in an American man-o'-war when, in the *Alfred,* he had sailed under Commander-in-Chief Hopkins. The result of that voyage had been court-martials and dismissal of several officers experienced in merchant shipping but of no talent for sea fighting. Eileen's reply Noah had received just before sailing last August under John Paul Jones, newly made a captain, in the *Providence.* She had returned to Rhode Island in October, but Noah had not got around to writing before, transferred to the *Alfred,* he again sailed on November second.

Eileen, though, had asked to hear from him again. She was home in Edenton, had had her sixteenth birthday, and wrote of a gay round of parties and balls. In a serious vein she begged Noah always to keep a sharp lookout for Angus MacAuliffe "who will never cease searching for you. Do not let him capture you, Noah, for 'twould mean terrible punishment. Even though you are now in the Navy, I fear he might lay hands on you if ever he can," she wrote.

Noah, after an opening paragraph, recounted his experiences up to now.

I am a year in the Navy and have seen much of our coast, the West Indies, and the North fishing grounds. Indeed, we are now off New England, homebound from Nova Scotia after 6 weeks of raising Hob with His Majesty's shipping.

On our last cruise, as news may have reached you, Captain Jones accounted for 16 British vessels. These we captured from Jamaica to Newfoundland —ships, brigantines, sloops, and schooners. Captain Jones burned or otherwise destroyed 8 and placed prize crews on the remaining 8 and fetched them home. We were then in port less than a month and kept very busy signing new men and Training them.

I have made some good friends aboard. One is Tom Boyce, of Massachusetts. He is 2 years older and a bold fellow. There are several others I like, including Lieutenant Nathaniel Fanning, a very Fair-Minded man and a splendid Officer. Red Cherry, an Indian, is a hardy fighter and a good seaman. And there are two Negroes, named Scipio and Cato. I suspect they are escap'd even as I am. But they never will discuss it and only show their fine teeth and roll their eyes.

When you heard last July about the Declaration of Independence, were you wild with Joy? And no doubt celebrated properly at last severing Ourselves from England? I understand Mr. Thos. Jefferson wrote the Document and 'twas changed a word here and there by Dr. Franklin. I wish I could write something so well and admire both Gentlemen very much. As to celebrating, we sailors heard of it in

August returning to port. Then we celebrated well. For at last the Colonies have held Thumb to Nose at the King and said, 'We no longer belong to you. We are our own Masters!' Which is a doctrine I much esteem. And Captain Jones says we shall now act united and become a great Nation.

Yet from such news as comes on vessels we capture, the war seems to be going ill. Gen'l Washington does not have monies and supplies; the Congress seems to talk but seldom Do; and the British with their great numbers of Men have steadily driv'n back our Armies. Now we have lost New York. We have suffered Military disaster on Long Island. And we lost the Forts on the Hudson River. It seems all our Armies do is Retreat. But none blame Gen'l Washington, who is a valiant fighter; but no man can win battles with only strategy for arms.

Nor is our Navy in much better plight. At the beginning, members of Congress gained commissions for friends and relatives and many were cowards and incompetents. Mr. Jos. Hewes of N. Carolina secured a Lieutenancy for Mr. Jones, and 'twas a blessing for America he did. For now he is Capt. Jones and his Ventures are greatly above all other Navy officers. Almost, he is head of the Navy—at least so far as battles fought are concerned.

But I must briefly outline our Encounters this voyage. We set out with 2 vessels, the Alfred *and*

Providence. *But at once the* Providence, *Capt. Hacker, gave us the slip, whether from cowardice I do not know. Capt. Jones's wrath was like a blazing fire, but he determined to carry on his Intentions with but our crew of 150 on the* Alfred.

Off Arcadie we engaged the Mellish, *40 guns. The Redcoats fought well but Capt. Jones out-maneuvered them and they surrendered. On the* Mellish *we found 1,000 complete soldiers' uniforms for Gen'ls Carleton & Burgoyne. And as I hear Gen'l Washington's men freeze for want of proper clothes, these will be Welcome.*

Though incommoded with Prisoners, we next descended on the coast of Arcadie which is in northern latitudes. We burned a transport and many warehouses. Capt. Jones desired to rescue 100 American prisoners at Isle Royale; however, the Harbor was frozen and we could not. In disappointment, we cruised the coast, capturing many small vessels and doing much Audacious Destruction. Capt. Jones fights with a handful of men as well as some admirals with thousands.

Off homeward, we encountered the frigate Milford, *48 guns. She was too heavy for us to Attack with so few seamen left after giving them to be Prize Crews, and with so many Prisoners in our hold. And Capt. Jones desired to protect the captured* Mellish *with the 1,000 uniforms and many captives. So as night drew her dark Curtains, we ran up a light on a halyard, as if for our prizes to follow. This attracted the* Milford, *whose stupid Capt. pursued us. Our prizes, of course, sailed another Direction. All night the* Milford *sought to engage us, we always eluding. In the morning there was a serious engagement. I served in a Long Tom gun crew and rec'd a piece of shell in my shoulder but will be in good health again ere long. With great shrewdness Capt. Jones finally put the* Alfred *to windward where we could rake the* Milford *thoroughly though she is a greater fighting Ship by far. Then we made good our escape, though our* Alfred *was leaking and we had many Wounded.*

It is in this situation I write now, with my left shoulder bandaged but not hurting much. We have but 2 days' water and rations remaining. But Capt. Jones saved our Prizes from the Milford's *capture—and, I may add, saved our necks as well.*

So, Eileen, as you divine, I like serving in the Navy though 'tis harder than the farm work I formerly did. Yet my companions are stout Fellows and though our Officers and Capt. are strict, they are Just. We often want warmth while at sea, and our pay when on land, and get neither. But to help our fair country become Free like the Declaration of Independence proclaims, then someone must suffer at least a little.

Ah! I now can see the coastline. Word is that we are putting in to Boston Harbor. I trust this letter finds you in good health and spirits and if it does not reach you by Christmas, at least I hope you enjoy a Merry one.

Will you write me in care of the Navy Office, Boston? A sailor does not know how long he has in Port, so I may be gone ere your reply comes, but 'twill be forwarded. I am in hopes we may meet again and in good health and circumstances. Goodbye, Eileen—

Noah Carr
Alfred *Sloop of War*
Off Boston, Dec. 12, 1776.

CHAPTER ELEVEN

THE SHADOW OF THE PAS

Noah Carr sat cross-legged on the
in the sailors' lodginghouse in Ports
of trousers was spread over his lap a
pinched in concentration he worke
patch over a worn place in one leg.

Awkwardly plying his needle, he
paid more heed to Mammy Fanny
MacAuliffe's plantation in Virginia.
him to darn his thick wool socks bu
patching was more difficult, and Noa
not listened carefully.

"You ain't got no missus to fix
Mammy Fanny warned, "and you ai
jus' th'ow 'em away. So watch her
Noah, 'cause you gwine need to kno

As he worked, he wondered how
were, and whether the war had take
Auliffe from home so as to give the
in his absence. Alleged to know ab
nance, MacAuliffe might have fou
well-paid post somewhere—that is, if
actually were with the Patriots. So
had never been able to feel at ease

CHAPTER ELEVEN

THE SHADOW OF THE PAST

Noah Carr sat cross-legged on the floor of his room in the sailors' lodginghouse in Portsmouth. A pair of trousers was spread over his lap and with brows pinched in concentration he worked at sewing a patch over a worn place in one leg.

Awkwardly plying his needle, he wished he had paid more heed to Mammy Fanny back on Angus MacAuliffe's plantation in Virginia. She had taught him to darn his thick wool socks but mending and patching was more difficult, and Noah knew he had not listened carefully.

"You ain't got no missus to fix yoah clothes," Mammy Fanny warned, "and you ain't so rich you jus' th'ow 'em away. So watch here now, Massa Noah, 'cause you gwine need to know."

As he worked, he wondered how she and Zel were, and whether the war had taken Angus MacAuliffe from home so as to give the Negroes peace in his absence. Alleged to know about naval ordnance, MacAuliffe might have found himself a well-paid post somewhere—that is, if his sympathies actually were with the Patriots. Somehow, Noah had never been able to feel at ease on that score.

Ah! I now can see the coastline. Word is that we are putting in to Boston Harbor. I trust this letter finds you in good health and spirits and if it does not reach you by Christmas, at least I hope you enjoy a Merry one.

Will you write me in care of the Navy Office, Boston? A sailor does not know how long he has in Port, so I may be gone ere your reply comes, but 'twill be forwarded. I am in hopes we may meet again and in good health and circumstances. Goodbye, Eileen—

Noah Carr
Alfred *Sloop of War*
Off Boston, Dec. 12, 1776.

Staring into space, he hoped he would never meet the man again—at least not until he was twenty-one. After that MacAuliffe could do him no harm save perhaps sue in civil court for damages suffered because he hadn't had Noah's labor during the full indenture period.

"If ever he sues me, I'll flatten his red nose for satisfaction!" he vowed. "But I'd much rather never lay eyes on the man again."

The door opened and Tom Boyce walked in. A brawny Irish lad of twenty, Tom was ruddy-faced and blue-eyed. In more than one action at sea Noah had found him a whirlwind fighter, afraid of nothing. The shipmates had struck up a warm friendship, and Noah thought there was no truer heart in the American Navy.

Tom closed the door. "Ho, tailor! Why don't you light a fire? 'Tis frosty here as standin' crow's-nest watch off Newfoundland. This is December, man. Did you think it July?"

"We've been ashore so long I scarce know what month it is. And we've no funds for firewood," Noah reminded. "Unless you walk over to Portsmouth Common and hew us down a fine tree."

"And be clapped in jail for't." Tom opened his coat and spilled on the iron bed. "This waitin'!" he grumbled. "Faith, how are we to rid the seas of Redcoats if we stay hidin' in harbor? When, oh, *when* do we sail?"

"I doubt Captain Jones can answer that. Though the *Ranger's* near ready at last."

"Two months we've rotted in Portsmouth. And before that, all summer in Boston. Out of coin we were in a week or two, and starvin' ever since. Except when we worked," Tom acknowledged wryly. "And we wouldn't have got to this town only the Captain paid the way to bring us. Congress wants us to fight, yet they send no money," he complained.

"Doubtless they have little. And they've been busy eluding General Howe. I'll wager Congress is embarrassed for fleeing Philadelphia, now we know Howe didn't mean to capture it at all. But for Captain Jones," Noah reflected, plying his needle, "there'd scarce be a Navy."

"Aye, mate. And to top it all, there he was fifth from the top in number of his commission. Then that thickheaded Congress suddenly names thirteen friends and relatives to have seniority over him!"

"I was his orderly when that news came," Noah remembered. "He was furious. If Congress had been within reach, I think he'd have torn them limb from limb. 'Twas politics, nothing else."

"Then the trouble about the *Amphitrite,*" Tom reminded with a yawn. "Aware they'd treated him ill, they sought to make amends with a special mission to France. So they said, 'Johnny, you take command of the *Amphitrite* that's just brought supplies.' But she's a French vessel and her captain won't give her up. More bungling!"

Noah bit off his thread and examined his work. "At least he finally got the *Ranger*. She's brand-new and I'll wager she can sail."

"So can a washtub, mate. But he's had to refit her and that's taken months. Why, the mains'l was only bent on yesterday. And I doubt we've a spare one in the locker. How can a man-o'-war put to sea without extra sails?" Tom demanded in disgust.

There was silence. Often they had discussed these matters, but the boredom of their wait for action was relieved somewhat by reviewing them once more.

"While we lie on our beam ends," Tom Boyce went on, "our farmer-soldiers are busy losing the war. But I doubt they get paid oftener than we, poor devils."

"And they face trained regiments with all the rations and guns needed. And mercenaries like those Hessians—Germans hired out to the King's officers to fight against Americans."

"Yes, things are black, Noah. With General Burgoyne sweepin' down from Canada with an army I'm told is irresistible. He means to join Clinton in New York and pinch off our whole north seaboard. Includin' General Washington's ragamuffin army."

Tom Boyce sighed. "When," he growled, beating his fist on the bed, "are we puttin' to sea? *When?*"

Noah was folding his mended trousers when a knock came on the door.

Tom, without rising, called, "If you're collectin' the rent, we ain't home. If you're frinds bringin' good tidings, come in!"

The door opened on two grinning Negroes, Cato and Scipio.

"Gen'lemen!" Cato saluted.

"We got big news!" Scipio, as thin and wiry-looking as his undersize partner, grinned.

Tom Boyce jerked upright. "*Good* news? Are we sailin'?"

"Quick as we kin pipe de crew. Den we gwine sail!"

"And dat ain't all," Scipio put in eagerly. "We gwine sail carryin' news—great *big* news. We gwine take it to France and tell de King, 'Looka heah, King Louie, what us Amuricans done-did. How we done whup de Redcoats out o' dey britches!'" Scipio tucked thumbs in his weskit, and rolling his eyes, strutted about the room. "We gwine say, 'King, how you like dat? Now you gwine send help? So we beat dem Redcoats worse an' chase 'em back home? 'Cause dey your enemies, King Louie, jus' like ours.' We gwine tell him—"

"Hold on!" Noah looked from one to the other

of the boys. "What big news are you talking about?"

The two Negroes exchanged wide grins. They came smartly to attention.

"Gen'lemen," Cato announced as officially as he could manage, "Gen'l Burgoyne done surrender. He done give up his whole army to Gen'l Gates!"

Tom's jaw dropped. "*What!*"

"General Burgoyne s-surrendered? To General Gates?" Noah stuttered.

"*Wowie!*" Tom leaped to his feet and began an Indian dance.

"Hold on, Tom! Are you certain?" Noah demanded.

As if in answer there came a sharp knock on the door. Cato opened it and the four sailors jerked to attention at sight of Second Lieutenant Nathaniel Fanning in the corridor. He wore sidearms, Noah noted, indicating that he was on duty.

"At ease, men." The second officer of the *Ranger* smiled as he motioned two sailors with him to wait in the corridor while he stepped into the room. "I see you've heard the news. It's the finest thing that's happened to our side in the war. Yes,"—he nodded to Noah and Tom's incredulous looks—"General Gates maneuvered Burgoyne into a trap. Cut off his supplies, had him helpless. There was nothing for our proud enemy to do but yield, and with him his entire army. It means New England is saved!"

Noah gave a low whistle. Sobering, he waited.

"This is a closely guarded secret, men, even though it seems to have gone like wildfire through our crew. The *Ranger* sails in a few hours, carrying this news to France where, as you know, Doctor Franklin has long tried to win support for the Colonies."

He waited while the men expressed their delight. "Boyce, you and Scipio and Cato report to the *Ranger* in an hour. Carr, you will accompany me rounding up the crew."

A few minutes later Noah, with the Indian, Red Cherry, and two other seamen, marched behind Lieutenant Fanning through the streets of Portsmouth. In pairs they entered every taproom and tavern seeking crewmen of the *Ranger*.

Presently Lieutenant Fanning had added another man to his detail.

"You, Carr, and Red Cherry, take Queen Anne Street," he instructed. "Search every likely place—lodginghouses, taprooms, and all. We've a hundred and forty men signed on but we've located only ninety-seven. We'll have to work faster. Mason and Knowles, you search the lower wharves. Ginrick, you come with me. We'll try the inns where some of the lads have been working while they await the call."

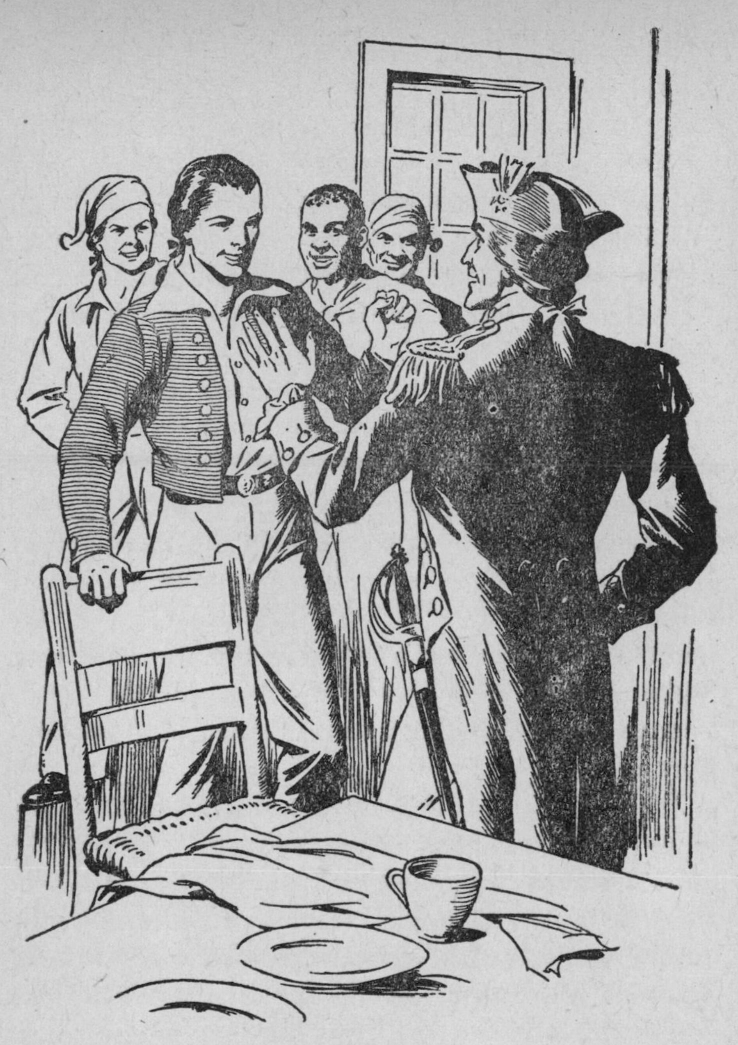

Lieutenant Fanning Spread the Good News

With the tall, uncommunicative Red Cherry striding quietly beside him, Noah began a search of Queen Anne Street. Into every public place they went, stores, taprooms, and lodginghouses. When a man in sailor's attire was found they asked his name, then consulted the list supplied by Lieutenant Fanning. If the list showed him a crewman of the *Ranger* he was ordered to report in one hour to the ship.

It was slow work, for two idle months in Portsmouth had scattered the crew. They had been signed on in Boston last spring, then given no duty all summer. Two months ago Captain Jones had brought them here expecting to sail as soon as stores could be brought aboard his new command, the *Ranger*. But the vessel was not yet finished, and while the Captain and a handful of officers labored night and day to prepare her, most crewmen had been forced to support themselves ashore as best they could.

Dissatisfied with the *Ranger*, Captain Jones had supervised structural changes in her. Then he replaced her too-heavy armament of 26 guns with 18 six-pounders. This done, he kept spurring the ship chandlers to deliver gear of all kinds, from pitch to sails. Since they received cash for outfitting privateers intended to raid British shipping along the American coast, the chandlers kept dodging their Navy work which paid only in drafts of questionable value on the Continental Congress. But now, at last, the *Ranger* was ready for sea.

"Your name, sailor?" Noah asked a brindle-complexioned man found mopping a taproom floor.

The other leaned on his mop-handle. "What affair is it of yours?"

"I need your name to find out if you're on this list. If you aren't on it, no harm done. If you are, we've a message for you. What did you say your name is?"

"I didn't say. And I won't." The other resumed his mopping.

"Just a minute, mate." Noah laid a hand on his shoulder. "If you won't tell us, we must assume you're on our list and trying to avoid recognition. In that case we'll arrest you and take you to our master-at-arms."

The fellow wrenched away. "I been willin' all summer to fight. Now I got a job and I want to keep it. I've starved and waited till I'm tired of it. I'll stay here and work so I can eat. On your way!" he ended roughly.

"I see him before," Red Cherry nodded to Noah. "He have name—uhm—Staley, maybe. He our man."

Abruptly Staley flung down his mop. He was starting away when Red Cherry's powerful hand on his arm halted him. Noah, consulting his list, checked the name with his stub of pencil.

"We're ready to sail, Staley. If you've been wanting to fight, now is your chance. It's no use to—"

"Let me alone! I've got a job and I want—"

"Arrest him, Red Cherry," Noah cut in.

As the Indian stepped behind Staley and gripped both his arms, the sailor yielded.

"You sure we're really sailin'?" he growled. "You sure?"

"It's only a matter of hours. And you'll hear news that'll be music to your ears. Give me your word you'll report, Staley," he offered, "and we'll let you go."

The man considered. "I'll report. I'm a seaman anyhow," he growled, eying with contempt his former work. "I'm no tavern-swabbin' landlubber!" He broke into a grin. "You don't blame me, do you, mates?"

"We have wait' long time. But now we sail," Red Cherry agreed. "He is gunner," he informed Noah. "Can shoot six-pounder, hit apple off tree."

"Let's move on, Red Cherry. We'll see you aboard, Staley."

"See you aboard, mates!"

As he and Red Cherry left the taproom Noah did not blame the gunner for at first resisting the call to arms. There had been similar calls, each proving false; and meanwhile the *Ranger's* men had sought jobs out of sheer necessity of eating. It was to their credit that more of them had not slipped away on privateers where twice the pay was offered, but had waited loyally for Captain Jones.

Red Cherry went first out of the taproom into the street. Noah, turning to close the door in his wake, heard an exclamation but gave it little heed. He turned front and took a step to join the Indian a few paces in advance—then halted as a heavy-set individual blocked his way.

Their eyes clashed. Noah's muscles went watery.

It was Angus MacAuliffe, whom he had last seen at the Virginia House in Fredericksburg more than two years since.

"So I've found ye!" the planter exulted. "Thought we'd never meet again, I doubt not? 'Specially so far from—"

The roaring in Noah's ears prevented hearing the rest. Incredulous, he stood with lips parted, staring at the familiar blotchy-red face of the man who was his master.

Impulse made him jerk back. Instantly MacAuliffe's hard stubby fingers sank into his shoulder. "No ye don't! Ye won't get away a second time, ye rascally bound-boy! I'll teach ye—"

Red Cherry's swooping hand wrenched MacAuliffe's away. "Take off!" the Indian barked.

MacAuliffe's eyes blazed. "You—you wampum warrior, don't ye touch me! Don't ye interfere!"

Noah gestured to Red Cherry to desist. He returned Angus MacAuliffe's glare unflinchingly.

"Yes," he acknowledged, "we've met again. But I don't wish any traffic with you, Mr. MacAuliffe."

"Oh, ye don't, eh? Well, I do with you, sir! Do ye forget you're a bound-boy till you're twenty-one? Do ye forget ye fled the home I provided for ye? That there's a price on your head? I'll have you taken in, my fine-feathered—"

"No," Noah interrupted calmly. "At least not until my term of service in the American Navy has ended."

"Navy? Service? You mean you—"

"I have the honor to be serving, yes. And as I'm about to sail, I'm afraid you will have to wait for a later meeting." Despite his cool exterior, Noah was seething with doubt that what he said was true. Though it doubtless would be valid if Lieutenant Fanning were here.

"That's no balk to my claim," MacAuliffe sneered. "You were an escaped bound-boy before you became a deck-swabber in the Navy. Here—constable!" he shouted across the street.

As the blue-uniformed individual opposite paused, then started toward them, Red Cherry inclined his head meaningly. He was suggesting that Noah flee, and for an instant impulse was wild within him to do so. But it would be too easy to trace him to the

Ranger.

"This boy is indentured to me until he's twenty-one," MacAuliffe informed the constable. "He fled my home in Virginia, and I've just caught him. I demand that you take him under arrest."

The constable studied them both. He chewed his tobacco, then squirted brown juice into the street. "That true, son? You indentured to him?"

Noah's eyes fell. "Yes."

"But he sailor. He on *Ranger* with Captain Jones. She sail quick," Red Cherry interposed. "No time for arrest."

"Bein' a sailor won't get him off! He was a bound-boy long before he was a sailor. So you're on Captain Jones's vessel, eh?" the planter sneered. "S'pose you know he murdered one of his crew in Tobago years back? Had to flee to escape hanging. But I guess you're two of a kind. Well?" he demanded of the constable.

The officer chewed and spat into the street. "Want the Injun too?"

"No. But I want this boy, Noah Carr!"

The constable slipped his arm through Noah's. "Come along. I got a good, tight jail a-waitin' fer you."

CHAPTER TWELVE

A VILLAIN'S TRUE COLORS

It was, as the constable said, a good, tight jail. Certainly it looked solid enough to Noah, pacing back and forth in his cell. It was a small stone building with but few cells, and at the moment he was the only prisoner. The jailer, a big man with a bulging stomach, spent his time in the little office at the front, his feet on the desk while he dozed asthmatically.

All afternoon Noah had been there. He had sought to reason with the jailer, first appealing for a quick hearing and when this failed, to the man's patriotism. "I've got to sail!" he insisted. But the jailer seemed unimpressed and waddled away.

It was growing dark, Noah saw through the single iron-barred window. Nervously he resumed his pacing. The tide would be coming in, and the *Ranger* might sail any moment now. And for France! Somehow, he felt that the most exciting cruise of all was coming—and he would miss it.

Disgustedly, he pounded one fist into the other palm. What had become of Red Cherry? He had thought the Indian would help him somehow. Of course Red Cherry had to report aboard, and perhaps his account of Noah's capture had failed to rouse Lieutenant Fanning's interest. After all, the ship must sail whether lacking one hand or not. Or perhaps Lieutenant Fanning felt there was nothing he could do. And doubtless Red Cherry could not get away from his duties to help Noah.

He stood thinking hard. It was not pleasant to picture himself traveling all the way to Virginia in custody of Angus MacAuliffe—and chained, doubtless, lest he escape again. There was nothing to look forward to as a captive except abuse and blows and at last, when they reached the plantation, the long-promised flogging.

"He'll give it to me himself," Noah muttered. "I'll be lucky if I live through it. The man hates me!"

For the twentieth time he gripped the window bars and sought futilely to shake them. But even if they could be dislodged, the window itself was too small to permit him to wriggle through.

Standing in the darkening cell, he searched it again in hope of inspiration that might help him effect an escape. It seemed Red Cherry was not free to come to his aid—and perhaps the ship had already sailed. If Noah was to break out of this jail he would have to think of the means and accomplish it alone.

He began to pace up and down again, then halted. Thoughtfully he kicked the sawdust littering the floor. His eyes played speculatively on the pail containing water for both drinking and washing.

In one stride Noah reached the stool beside his bunk. He removed a boot, then one sock. He pulled his boot back on and leaning, scooped handfuls of sawdust and crammed them into his sock. He worked thus until the foot of the sock was packed hard. Holding it by its ankle part, he plunged it into the pail of water. Noah waited until the sawdust was well soaked. Lifting it out, he tried its weight. A hopeful grin quirked the corners of his mouth and for good measure he immersed the sock once more.

Then he went to the barred door of his cell. "Jailer!" he called in a tone indicating pain. "Hello there! Jailer!"

At first it brought no response. Noah shouted louder, and a sleepy inquiry floated back. At last the man got to his feet and came shuffling along the corridor, his lantern held shoulder-high.

"What's wrong? What do ye want?"

"Fetch a doctor, quick! *Oh!*" Noah held both hands to his stomach and bent over, simulating great pain. "I've got awful cramps. *Oh!*" he groaned again.

"Eh? Cramps? Come, you can't trick me!" But he held his light the better to see Noah, and stepped nearer the barred door. "Hmm—ye do look in pain. But there's no doctor this time of—"

"Do something, can't you? *Oh! Oh!*" Noah went

into another series of groans.

He leaned against the door as if pain prevented his standing upright. The jailer scratched his great paunch indecisively.

Abruptly Noah reached between the bars. He grabbed the man's shirt, and jerking him closer, thrust his other hand between bars and lifted his homemade club. Before the jailer could so much as cringe, the heavy, wet, sawdust-packed sock struck his forehead with a dull thud. Again it hit, and a third time.

The weapon was surprisingly effective. The man's eyes fluttered shut. He sighed, his knees buckling. His lantern spilled from his hand and went clattering to the floor. With a low moan he collapsed in a heap.

Noah stared at him. The lantern lay on its side and its candle would soon go out. As he fell, the jailer had toppled away from the cell door. Stooping, Noah reached between bars for the man's clothing, to drag him close enough to extract the heavy iron cell-key from his pocket.

His fingers touched the fellow's shirt but insufficiently to grasp it. Noah withdrew his arm, got on his knees, and thrust his arm between bars until they gouged his shoulder. His anxious fingers could grasp a little of the fellow's shirt now and he pulled.

The cloth ripped away. The jailer, insensible, remained tantalizingly out of reach.

Noah was perspiring now. He readjusted his position and again strained his reach, unaware that in his anxiety he was grunting with the effort. But no—he could not quite get sufficient hold on the man's clothing to drag him nearer.

He sat back panting. His brain whirled with speculation: how was he to haul the jailer close enough to get his key? Again he tried, but again met defeat.

Any moment now the jailer would regain consciousness. Noah stared around his cell, seeking a suggestion, some tool to use. But he found none. In wrathful chagrin he got up, mopping his brow with his sleeve. He was so close to escape, yet so far!

The hoot of an owl drew his notice. Darting to the cell window, Noah imitated the call. Out of the dark a figure appeared, and with vast relief he recognized Red Cherry.

"We come get you. Tom here too," the Indian whispered.

"Thank heaven! Hurry to the front, then come back to my cell." Hurriedly he reported how he had struck the jailer insensible.

The lantern candle was flickering out as Tom Boyce and Red Cherry came trotting down the corridor. Quickly Red Cherry searched the jailer's pockets, found the key, and unlocked the cell door.

"What did ye hit him with, a shillelah?"

"Tie him up," suggested Red Cherry. "Put him in cell, yes?"

"Yes. And let's hurry!"

In a few moments the jailer, bound hand and foot and gagged, lay on the floor of Noah's cell. The three locked its door, then hurried to the office. Noah tossed the key on the floor and with a wry grin followed his mates outside.

"Are we sailing soon?"

"The Captain didn't confide exactly when," Tom Boyce replied. "However, we'd better get aboard, for 'twon't be long. They were takin' on the last fresh water when Red Cherry and I slipped away. That Lieutenant Fanning," he added irritably as the three hurried along the street, "wasn't satisfied with one roll call. No! He had to have two."

"We turn at corner. Make shorter way," suggested the Indian.

"I'm obliged to you for coming," Noah declared. "I was beginning to see myself back in Virginia, my wrists tied to a tree branch, and Mr. MacAuliffe flogging me so—"

The words died in his throat. They had approached a tavern and were almost passing its entrance when the door opened and revealed against yellow light within the very man he had named.

He halted. The others continued, not comprehending for an instant. They glanced back to see

Noah step to the curb and stand facing the street as if idling there. His back was to Angus MacAuliffe. The planter, apparently thinking of something else, stood a moment as if undecided in which direction to go.

Apprehensive lest he be recognized, Noah turned and walked back the way he had come. In an instant Tom Boyce and Red Cherry overtook him.

"Dear man, what's got into—" Boyce began.

"Ssh! That was Mr. MacAuliffe came out of the tavern. I don't want to see him!"

"Hivenly day, I should think not." Boyce glanced over his shoulder. "The bloody ruffian's followin' us!"

"He come our way," verified Red Cherry.

Anxiety rose in Noah and he walked faster. The others assured him grimly that if Angus MacAuliffe so much as called out his name they would whirl and pounce on him.

"We'll beat his head to a pulp! Faith, let's do't and be done!"

"No, Tom. It might draw a crowd and we'd all end up in jail. Are you sure he's following us?" He did not want to look around lest he be recognized.

"Not sure. Maybe," Red Cherry voiced his thought.

"We'll turn this corner, then." They did so, entering a darker street. The three came to an alley, and finding that MacAuliffe seemed not to have reached the corner, darted into its friendly darkness.

"Let's wait a bit." Noah could not suppress a shiver. "Not ten minutes after I leave jail, I run into that man again! But he didn't know me," he reflected, "or he'd have raised a hue and cry."

At Red Cherry's low warning the three shrank back against a stone wall. Dimly outlined at the alley street entrance was Angus MacAuliffe. He stood as if considering; then slowly he entered the alley toward them.

"Never fear. We'll nab him!" Boyce whispered.

Next instant they sighted another figure dimly silhouetted in the alley opening. That man, like MacAuliffe, gazed up and down the street; then he too came into the alley.

The three shrank into its corner, for the alley was a blind one and they could go no farther. It was too dark now to see either MacAuliffe or the man who had followed, but in a moment they heard the planter's voice.

"Sergeant?"

"Ssh! Don't call me Sergeant!"

"All right. But we're safe here; there's no one about. It didn't look safe in that tavern to me. Did you notice that fellow watching when—"

"He wasn't thinking of you or me either. Why should anyone suspect? You're nervous."

"Of course I'm nervous. Do you think I relish this

spy work? If any hotheaded Patriot caught me at it I wouldn't need an hour to swing from a gallows. And for what you're paying, I'm perhaps a fool to serve!"

"You're not serving me. You're serving His Majesty. Now calm down, MacAuliffe. Tell me what you have and we'll be off."

"I'll tell you when I feel the money. Not before!"

The unknown man grunted irritably. "Here 'tis. Ten pound, you get. I suppose you'll have to count it like the last time. I'll put a spark to this taper. Wait."

There was sound of a flint scratching. A low flame started on the taper the man called Sergeant held. He handed something to MacAuliffe, who swiftly examined it. The taper went out.

"All right. But ten pound's little enough. My neck's worth more than that," he complained.

"Your neck! What about mine? Do I get ten pounds? I've only a soldier's pay. Well," the other said in annoyance, "what's your news?"

"Captain John Paul Jones sails tonight in the 'Ranger.' For France."

"Is that all? Everyone in Portsmouth knows that! Have you got his course? We'll want to nab that pirate and teach him a thing or two!"

"Yes, I have his course. I was aboard his vessel but two hours since. I'll tell it slow so you'll remember. Then I'll repeat it. Ready?"

Tom Boyce's lips were close to Noah's ear. "Faith, we'll not permit that! Let's set on the traitors!"

"Right. When I give the signal." Noah nudged Red Cherry, whose answering nudge proved he understood.

The three crept stealthily forward. Red Cherry was in the lead and but for the faint dark mass of his body Noah would not have believed anyone there, so utterly silent did he move.

MacAuliffe was giving the course the *Ranger* was expected to follow to elude the King's men-o'-war lying in wait off the coast. Noah made out his figure and that of the man he called Sergeant.

"*Now!*"

Red Cherry leaped on the sergeant. Noah sprang for MacAuliffe but found him already reeling under Tom Boyce's maul-like blow. Noah struck out, though, and felt his fist encounter the planter's chin. MacAuliffe, reeling and groggy, instinctively sought to defend himself.

"Go to it! He's yours!" Tom cried.

Noah felt the planter's hard knuckles graze his temple. He waded in with left and right fists swinging at the man's face. Angus MacAuliffe backed a step, found wall behind him, and suddenly tried to whirl sideways and run. Noah's foot shot out. With a grunt MacAuliffe tripped and sprawled on his face in the muddy alley.

Boyce and Noah were on him like cats. "What'll—we—do with 'em?" Noah panted, aware that Red Cherry had knocked his man senseless almost at the first blow.

"Now that's a question." Tom Boyce stooped, and seizing MacAuliffe's hair, turned his face sideways. "My dear sir, do ye know who 'tis sittin' on ye? Seaman Noah Carr of the American Navy. And don't yell out lest ye want to die!" Tom pressed the point of his sheath-knife to the planter's throat.

"You—you—!" MacAuliffe was speechless with rage. "You rascally bound-boy, you broke jail and—"

"That's it!" Noah exclaimed. "Look, fellows: why not leave these traitors in jail? It's only a block from here. We can't turn 'em loose or they'll go on with their dirty work. So let's leave 'em there, where they'll be secure!"

Red Cherry grunted approval. Tom Boyce chuckled and held his knife to MacAuliffe's neck while Noah got off the man, straightening.

"Now get up. If ye make one bad move," Boyce warned, shifting his knife to the back of his neck, "I'll stick this in so it'll come out your Adam's apple!"

Angus MacAuliffe's silence proved him properly respectful. Red Cherry, meanwhile, had lifted the sergeant to his feet and was slapping the man's face to bring him fully conscious. Noah went to peer

Noah Struck Hard at the Planter's Chin

at him, but thought he had not seen him before.

"So you're one of His Majesty's spies? We'll do our best to give you hospitality, Sergeant."

Still dazed, the man did not reply. "Red Cherry, can you take care of him?" As the Indian grunted, Noah went on: "I'll go to the street entrance and see if it's clear. Wait."

A few moments later the five were walking along the street, Angus MacAuliffe close in front of Tom Boyce with the sailor's knife point pricking the back of his neck, and the sergeant between Noah and Red Cherry. The Indian's knife point in the small of the captive's back was ample warning for him to behave.

They reached the jail and, reconnoitering, Noah found no change since their departure. The jailer still lay bound in Noah's cell, indicating that his escape had not become known to anyone else.

"Let's give them each a cell," he suggested, picking up the discarded key. "We'll tie and gag them and leave a note on the jailer's desk. It'll state that Angus MacAuliffe is a traitor and that the sergeant here is a British soldier acting as a spy."

"Man, 'tis a lovely idea. We can use blankets to tie 'em and for gaggin,' too. Faith," Tom Boyce added, "we'd best hurry or Captain Jones'll be leavin' for France."

Noah and Boyce took care of MacAuliffe while

Red Cherry waited with his captive. His a
bound and his hands fastened behind him, M
Auliffe watched Noah with hate blazing in his ey

"You—you—!" he choked.

Noah returned his glare. "I was fearful of you till tonight, Mr. MacAuliffe. You were my master and I an escaped bound-boy. Not that my conscience bothered me," he assured him. "I worked faithfully for you back in Virginia, but you've no kindness, no decency, in your make-up. I fled your domination because I feared for my life."

"And rightly," MacAuliffe snarled. "I'd have flogged you to a corpse!"

"That's what I expected. But now," he went on, his lip curling, "I find you a traitor and I've no words to express my contempt. You, the naval ordnance expert! You sat in conferences with important men, pretending to be a great Patriot. And all the time you were selling our secrets for money!"

"You can't prove it. I'll have you flogged yet, mark my—" His words were muffled as Tom Boyce adjusted a strip of soiled blanket over his mouth.

"Go right on talkin', man," he invited as he fixed the knot. "Only from now on, I'm after thinkin' ye'll talk to yourself."

"Me ready." Red Cherry emerged from the next cell. "I fix him alone. He don't get away."

Noah glanced at the sergeant and smiled. "You

certainly did fix him good, Red Cherry. Lock their cell doors, boys. I'll go write the note in the office."

In a matter of minutes the note was written, explaining that Angus MacAuliffe had been nabbed while selling military secrets to the sergeant, a member of the King's Army. Request was made to give both prisoners over to military authorities for court-martial. Noah added explanation that the three signers were members of Captain Jones's crew and because it was sailing-time were unable to bring their accusations in person. Then he wrote his name and rank on the *Ranger* and handed the quill to Red Cherry. The Indian made an *x* and gave the quill to Tom Boyce. Laboriously, his face screwed up, Tom traced out his name.

"Does that say 'Tom Boyce'? I niver learnt much writin'."

"It does. Now let's get to the ship!"

They hurried out of the jail and made for the wharves. Fog had settled over the harbor, but Tom and the Indian promptly located their rowboat. Dropping into it, the three shoved off. Noah was at the oars and directed the craft according to Tom's instructions from the bow.

Boyce chuckled. "Ye rascally bound-boy," he chided, "have ye no respect for your master? Leavin' him so uncomfortable so far from home!"

Red Cherry's grunt was as near as he ever came

to laughter. Noah, although he appreciated the humor of what they had done, was vastly relieved at his escape. He pulled hard at the oars, thankful too that he had nabbed a traitor. If word of the *Ranger's* course had reached the King's men-o'-war standing off New England it might have resulted in loss of the *Ranger* and perhaps of her entire crew—a very serious blow to America.

Somehow, he had never believed Angus MacAuliffe's heart was with the Colonies in their struggle for freedom. He understood now why the man had always been close-mouthed regarding his views. But instinct had kept warning Noah, though he'd no proof until tonight.

"Wait till Eileen learns this," he mused. Then as a thought struck him: "Boys, we must report exactly what happened to Captain Jones. He may want to alter his course."

"Report? Nay, I'll but sneak aboard as if I wasn't gone," Tom Boyce declared. "We'd no permission to leave, Red Cherry and I. And Lieutenant Fanning wouldn't look kindly on our departin' silently over the side. He'd have some ugly word for't like desertion."

He grunted. "Sure, and we would have this soupy fog!"

The smoke-like gray was closing them in. It was worse now, so thick that nothing could be seen a few boat-lengths away.

"Are we near the ship?" Noah asked.

"Faith, I expected her to be sittin' right here, but —It must be the pesky fog," Tom concluded. "Row gintly, man."

Noah complied. At word from the bow he again let their craft drift. Tom Boyce spoke softly. He was on his knees, peering ahead.

"I can't see her. I tell you the bloody ship was exactly here, anchored!"

"She was here," Red Cherry affirmed. "Too bad. She gone."

The three sat gripped with dismay. The Indian's sense of direction was virtually perfect. If Red Cherry said the *Ranger* had been at this spot, she had been. If he said she was gone . . .

Tom Boyce cried out in anger, "Blast them two traitors! They made us miss her. The 'Ranger's' on her way to France, mates. Without us!"

CHAPTER THIRTEEN

CAPTAIN JONES'S STORY

The three friends sat discouraged and silent in their drifting rowboat. Each was thinking how much he had wanted to sail in the *Ranger*. Undoubtedly there would be glorious sea battles, for Captain Jones's audacity guaranteed action. Equally important, the *Ranger* was carrying news of General Burgoyne's surrender of his entire army, the greatest triumph for the American States thus far. That triumph would be celebrated in France. And it gave hope of others soon stemming from it.

For this reason Benjamin Franklin, as American representative in Paris and Versailles, had striven for two years to persuade France to declare war against England. The succession of American army defeats had kept the French from such a declaration, much as their king disliked the British. News of General Burgoyne's surrender might bring France, with her great resources, into the war on America's side.

The French, of course, had already contributed much to the Patriots' fight for freedom, though unofficially. The French army officer General Lafayette was serving under General Washington. There was Rochambeau, and there were other

Frenchmen, titled men and common folk, who had left their homeland to fight for strangers' freedom. Supplies had come from the generous French people, such as those brought on the *Amphitrite*, the vessel which had almost passed to Captain Jones's command before he was given the *Ranger*.

"We'll miss raiding the English coast," Tom Boyce reminded them gloomily. "Captain Jones expects to do it from France."

"And 'Ranger' carry new flag," Red Cherry put in. "Old Continental flag with snake on it no more used. Congress pass resolution. Captain Jones first with new United States flag in foreign countries."

"United States flag? What's it like?" Noah asked.

"Very pretty. Has red stripes, white stripes, blue with stars on. One stripe for each colony, also one star. Is pretty flag. I saw when it brought aboard."

"We're not colonies any more," Tom explained. "We're the United States of America."

They lapsed into silence. The fog, Noah thought, was denser than before. Apparently there was no vessel moving in the Portsmouth roadstead for he could hear no creak of pulleys, no plashing of water. Like heavy, odorless smoke the fog made a fuzzy world of gray, so thick that Noah, twisting to look, could not see beyond Tom in the bow.

"*Say!*" he ejaculated.

"What? D'you see her?"

"No. But if we're lost in this fog, so must the 'Ranger' be!"

"You don't say?" Tom Boyce said wearily.

"But don't you catch on? Captain Jones probably welcomed fog—a little, anyhow, so as to slip out of harbor. But how can he take out a ship like the *Ranger* when he may collide with another vessel any instant? After waiting for months to sail," Noah rushed on, "do you think he'll risk a collision?"

"No pilot would take vessel now," Red Cherry agreed.

Tom gave a low whistle. "Ye mean she isn't gone?"

"Of course she hasn't gone. She slipped her anchor," Noah acknowledged, "but I'll wager five British generals against a cup of hard cider that the 'Ranger' had to anchor again. I tell you," he insisted, "if we can't find anything with a rowboat, a vessel like the 'Ranger' can't find her way out of port!"

The others hesitated. "You mean we'd better search?"

"That's just what I mean."

Tom Boyce sighed. "Me mother oft told me how thick me head is. I should've believed her. Faith, 'tis only good for sittin' a hat on!"

"Red Cherry, your eyes and ears are better than ours. You've an instinct for such things. You're in command. Find the 'Ranger!' "

The Indian listened for a long minute. Then he

directed Noah to row gently. Red Cherry and Tom Boyce had exchanged places, and, as he knelt in the bow, Red Cherry's remarkable heritage of trailing came into play.

"Stop! Wharf!"

Noah back-paddled. "Slow. More on starboard."

Thus it went, the small craft inching past pilings and wharf-ends and close under the hulls of anchored vessels. There was tension in the search, apprehension lest they strike something that would sink them. Should that happen, Noah reflected, he would not even know in which direction to swim for safety.

At a low word from Red Cherry, he let the rowboat drift. He felt a slight jar as the bow nosed into some obstruction. There was a pause. Noah felt rather than saw something looming high above; but as Red Cherry pushed their craft along the vague mass he decided it was another wharf. Perhaps even the Indian's senses, acute as they were, could not cope with fog that was as thick as—

"Here," whispered Red Cherry.

"He says 'here,'" Tom Boyce relayed guardedly. He turned to Red Cherry, then twisted back. "Hivenly days, the feathered heathen has *found* her. It's the—"

"Ssh!"

They sat silent. Now Noah vaguely made out the *Ranger's* stern. He heard the lazy grind of anchor chain in hawsehole, and, reaching out, touched the chain slanting steeply into the water. Above them came faint sounds of walking. The ship's bell sounded. A voice floated out to them saying:

"Sev-en bells! And all's well!"

"Except with us," Tom Boyce muttered. "How'll we get aboard without anyone knowin'? It's the brig and bread and water if we're caught—that is, assumin' we ain't been missed. I doubt the Captain'll want to pipe us aboard like we were admirals!"

The three huddled close. "Me go up chain," Red Cherry proposed. "Pretty soon drop rope. When I jerk, Tom come. Jerk again, Noah come. No let watch hear us. Let rowboat drift away."

This was agreed to. Maneuvering their craft silently, Noah grasped the anchor chain. He could scarcely hear and only vaguely see Red Cherry swing nimbly onto it and move upward.

A rope stung his shoulder, its end splashing softly in the water. Tom Boyce crouched, holding it. When he felt Red Cherry's jerk, he patted Noah's head in farewell, then vanished hand-over-hand.

Now Noah held the rope taut. It seemed a long wait until the reassuring jerk told him to come aboard. He tested his weight on the rope, found it solid, and swung cat-like away from the rowboat. Suppressing his hard breathing, he mounted in utter silence to the rail. He got one hand over, then the other, then his knee. An instant later he stood aboard the *Ranger*.

He sought Red Cherry and Tom, not daring to whisper a query. Deciding they were padding softly to the companionway amidships to go below, Noah moved in that direction. He rounded the after deck-house containing the officers' quarters and suddenly crouched beside a capstan as the deck-watch strolled past.

Judging it safe, he again moved cautiously forward. He decided to follow the rail lest he collide with something. Guided by his hand, he thought himself within a few steps of the companionway and turned from the rail.

"Who's that?"

Noah stood like a statue. A hand touched his chest, ran lightly down his side.

"Who is it?"

He gulped. It would not help to say he was the deck-watch for he did not know the man's name. Besides, he might get a mate into trouble.

"It's Seaman Carr, sir."

There was a pause. "So you decided to join us, after all?" Captain Jones inquired sarcastically. "I'm surprised at you, Carr. Tippling in some tavern, I doubt not, while Lieutenant Fanning depended on you to help round up the crew. Come to my quarters!"

"It's Seaman Carr, Sir."

Noah could not dislodge the lump in his throat. Apprehensively he followed the dark blur before him until a cabin door opening sprayed yellow light over Captain Jones's short, brawny form. The Captain descended into his cabin, Noah following and closing the door. Removing his cap, he stood at attention at the end of a table littered with charts.

Captain Jones's faded blue eyes were cold as ice and left a tremor in Noah as they scrutinized him from head to foot. He dropped in a chair.

"It's desertion to miss your sailing. You know that?"

Noah's eyes fell to the table. "Yes, sir. I didn't want to miss it, sir. But—"

"Who were your companions?"

"Companions, sir?" He tried to sound surprised.

"Yes, companions! You came up a rope. It didn't grow there. Someone aboard dropped it to you. And I doubt not that person came up the anchor chain, then spilled you the rope. If the watch weren't so stupid, he'd have seen what I saw and seized you. How many of you were there?"

"Three, sir."

"Who were the other two?"

Noah stared at the table. "Sir," he said, "I cannot be the cause of other men being punished. Especially when they were absent from duty to help me, so I could come aboard."

Captain Jones glared. But he seemed to know that Noah would not divulge the names of the others even under threat of severe punishment. He shifted his position in the chair. His eyes on Noah felt to the boy like crickets roving over his skin.

"They helped you, eh? What trouble were you in?"

"Sir, in seeking members of the crew I encountered Mr. MacAuliffe. He had me arrested and thrown in jail."

Captain Jones frowned. "You mean Mr. Angus MacAuliffe, who was your master in Virginia? The naval ordnance expert? Why–I'd forgotten that you and he– Hmm," he reflected. "The man's been aboard off and on concerning my change of gunnery. As late as this afternoon he still urged me to mount six more eight-pounders–more weight than she'll carry and still maneuver. But–"

"Sir, Mr. MacAuliffe is a spy for the British."

Captain Jones started violently. His eyes were piercing. "Carr, do you realize the seriousness of what you say?"

"Yes, sir, I do."

He pursed his lips in the reflective way he had. He sat down. "At ease, Noah–sit if you like." He gestured. "Now give me the full story. Everything. I believe you're an honest lad," he went on. "I liked you that day two or three years ago when I found you plowing on Mr. MacAuliffe's plantation. I liked you well enough at that Virginia House meeting, near Fredericksburg, to give you the pistol. I always sympathize with a man who's fighting for his freedom. And you've been a good seaman," he added. "Now, tell your story without the slightest exaggeration. Don't be afraid—but give me only facts!"

Noah told him. He started at the point where he and Red Cherry—though he said only "a mate"—were sent to gather members of the *Ranger's* crew. He told of meeting MacAuliffe, his arrest, his rescue; and of the accidental meeting again with MacAuliffe, and overhearing his talk with the British soldier in civilian disguise.

Captain Jones sat drumming his fingers on the table. His eyes scarcely left Noah's throughout the entire account.

"Your shipmates will verify this?"

"Indeed yes, sir. I don't want to be the cause of their punishment, Captain—"

"Forget that. This is too important; it far overshadows a routine matter of discipline." He thrust his legs out and crossed his ankles. "That black-hearted scoundrel! I never fully trusted him but thought 'twas because I disliked him. Yes?" he answered a knock on the door.

First Lieutenant Simpson entered. "Captain Jones, I believe the fog is lifting enough to take her out now."

"Good. Take– No," he caught himself, glancing at Noah. "Remain with us a few minutes, Mr. Simpson. Here." He seized paper and quill pen and began to write rapidly. Now and then he paused, thinking. Once he glanced at Noah.

"We could leave you to testify against him. No," he decided, his eyes twinkling, "you'd be disappointed at that after all your difficulty joining us."

"Yes, sir. Besides–er–I'm still indentured to Mr. MacAuliffe."

"Ah, yes. Even if he were convicted, you'd still be in trouble. As a fugitive, you know, if anyone wanted to bother you." He returned to writing and a moment later finished.

"Mr. Simpson, please listen to this. It is Seaman Carr's story. Noah, interrupt me if I've made any error."

He proceeded to read what he had written, a straightforward account just as Noah had given it to him of Noah's escape from the jail with the help of two friends, his overhearing of MacAuliffe and the British sergeant in the alley, and their capture.

"Is that the way it was, Noah?"

"Yes, sir, exactly."

Mr. Simpson's eyes showed his amazement. "Mr. MacAuliffe who has been aboard here so often? It's astounding! Shall I plot a different course,

Captain?"

"I think not, since the information hasn't got to the enemy. Noah, I'd like you to sign this." He offered the quill. "I want you to give me the names of your two associates. I shan't discipline them or scold them in the least. This is much too important by comparison. But we should have their signatures also."

Noah gave the others' names and presently Mr. Simpson returned with Red Cherry and Tom Boyce. They looked frightened until Noah quickly explained. Then the two signed, and, with relieved expressions, departed. Captain Jones folded the paper and handed it to Mr. Simpson.

"Send a man ashore to hand this to the officer in charge of the naval shore patrol, and have him urge the officer to deliver it at once to the shore commandant. We'll wait a reasonable time for the man to return. Then, if the fog is still thin enough, you may take the 'Ranger' out, Mr. Simpson."

The senior lieutenant retired. Noah, undecided as to whether he also had been dismissed, waited. Captain Jones motioned for him to resume his chair.

"I recall that you told me once your father died when you were small."

"Yes, sir. And I believe in my heart there was trickery about my indenture," Noah declared. "I can't prove it, for I have the paper in my chest below and it does look properly made out and signed."

"Then what makes you suggest trickery? Since you say the paper looks legal and all."

"Well, sir, two reasons. The first is, my mother had some wealth, I do believe. She never had to work, and we traveled a bit. Suddenly after her death I was a pauper and a bound-boy." Noah shook his head as if to drive haze from his brain. "I can prove nothing. But I feel very strongly, sir, that I was—well, meant to be a gentleman," he said earnestly.

"Hm. Many of us have dreams, Noah. Mere belief isn't much to go on. Your second reason?"

"We now know Mr. MacAuliffe's true stripe, sir—that he's no Patriot, but a Loyalist spy. If he'd stoop to spying, it's plain he's capable of any crookedness to his advantage. It makes me doubly of a mind there was trickery somehow about my indenture."

Captain Jones did not answer at once. "I hope you can prove that some day. I'll keep it in mind," he promised, "and if ever I can help, I shall do so."

"Thank you, Captain Jones."

The other scarcely heard him. He sat slouched down, his fingers idly tapping the table.

"I know what it is to have no father. I have none—less than you, even." He gazed at the ceiling. "I was raised by my mother on an estate at Kirkcudbright, Scotland. I disliked it and ran away to sea when I was fourteen. I had discovered," he explained sadly, "that my father seemed to be the nobleman who owned the estate. But I've no proof, and he'll never claim me."

Noah waited. The Captain went on as if to himself:

"Misfortune thus caught me early and has dogged me half around the world. When I was master of a vessel lying in Tobago, West Indies, a drunken carpenter tried to lead a mutiny. He came at me, and I defended myself with a sword. I struck him harder than I thought, and he died. Of course I gave myself up to the Governor, who advised me that no Court of Inquiry could be held for many months. He hinted I'd be a fool to rot in jail, waiting, since I was sure to be exonerated."

Again, silence.

"So I fled. Ever since, the story's been twisted out of all reality. The British call me a felon, a traitor, and a pirate. I've a black reputation, Noah."

"No, sir, not in America."

That won a brief smile.

"Even in America my past—though I'm blameless—has pursued me. In Virginia, because I'd sailed in the slave trade, I was looked down on socially. Every twist and turn of my life," he said gloomily, "has seemed to add to people's whispering about me. Even the girl I'd have wed—"

He checked himself. Noah, embarrassed, stared at the floor. In the long silence he heard muffledly the call of the watch. The *Ranger* was moving, he realized. He felt her lift to the first swells of the Atlantic on her way to France.

"So your lot has not been the only hard one on this planet," Captain Jones said, rising. As Noah swiftly got up he offered his hand. "We're birds of a feather, Noah. We'll have to carve our way to glory with our swords, for nothing is given to us as to some fortunate persons. But," he added grimly, "if we're ill-used today—well, history shall weigh us and not find us wanting!

"Good night," Captain Jones smiled a little sadly as Noah went out of the cabin.

CHAPTER FOURTEEN

ATTACKING THE ENEMY'S COAST

The wintry voyage to France required a month, and as Captain Jones wrote in his report it was "uneventful." Noah did not fully agree, since off the Azores the *Ranger* captured two brigantines out of Malaga, put prize crews aboard, and sent them to France for sale by American agents. A few days later ten British sail under strong convoy were sighted. Cleared for action, the *Ranger* sought to lure from her charges the largest man-o'-war Noah had yet seen.

But H.M.S. *Invincible* carried 74 guns to the *Ranger's* 18 and soon demonstrated her superiority. Keeping out of range of the smaller vessel, she shot away the Yankee's topmast and planted a shell below the waterline at her bow. For once Captain Jones was compelled to abandon a project.

This action delayed arrival of the *Ranger* in the River Loire off the French city of Nantes. Immediately, Tom Boyce and Bos'n Green were despatched with news of Burgoyne's surrender to Passy, near Paris, where Doctor Benjamin Franklin lived. Ruefully Tom explained on his return that Mr. John Loring Austen, a messenger from Congress, had arrived with the news two days earlier. Nor had Tom seen Doctor Franklin, busy with the two American commissioners who had joined him, Mr. Richard Henry Lee and Mr. Silas Deane.

Noah saw little of Nantes or French life, being kept busy aboard ship. Promoted to midshipman, a petty officer's rating, he had to assist in re-stationing the Long Toms. Captain Jones had found it necessary again to alter his vessel's ballast and to fit shorter masts in the hope of improving her sailing qualities.

As the work progressed, Noah, piecing together bits of talk, knew that Captain Jones hoped to command a fine man-o'-war being especially—and secretly—built for him in Holland. This vessel, the *Indien,* would be well-armed yet able to outsail the finest ship of the British fleet.

At last the *Ranger* was ready. Orders arrived from the three American commissioners and just at daybreak on April 10 the warship nosed her way out of the River Loire into the Atlantic. A week later Noah, wondering when he could mail his letter, wrote to Eileen MacAuliffe the events thus far:

None knew the Capt.'s plan but all felt certain he meant to scourge the English coast as he has so long wanted. It had been hoped we would have two Vessels, then Lt. Simpson would command this one and Capt. Jones the new one. But alas! she is not ready. And I must say Lt. Simpson acts Disgruntled, as if he already sees himself master here and takes it ill Capt. Jones is still aboard. Some of the crew grumble about it also, calling the Capt. a foreigner. It fair makes me boil, for many among us were not born in the Colonies. But who has won more Glory for America than Capt. Jones?

We were scarce at sea when we captured a brigantine carrying flaxseed to Ireland, and sank her. Three days later we took the Lord Chatham *laden with porter and Merchandise. We put a prize crew aboard and sent her to Brest.*

Next day the Capt. called us to assembly. He talked to us from the quarter-deck. "Men, we are going to show these English that Americans are brave fighters. You have all heard how ill they treat Americans taken prisoner. They keep them in dark dungeons or work them like slaves, feeding them little. And you all know how Redcoats have burned many American cities without cause.

"We are now in English home waters," the Capt. said. "I have brought you here to teach the lordly English a lesson.

"The prisoners we take," he went on, "our commissioners will offer to exchange so as to liberate American captives. And we shall do some burning along the enemy coast to prove that we also can play at that game."

As I learned later, when we entered the Firth of Forth we were close to shores where the Capt. was born. On the 18th at Eventide our small boats were manned to go ashore for a raid. But the wind changed, raising such a sea that we were Fortunate to escape being dashed on the rocks. On the 20th, after sinking two vessels meanwhile, we took two pilots off a fishing craft. They told us the sloop Drake, *20 guns, was at anchor in Belfast Lough.*

Our Capt. at once planned to come stealthily up to the Drake's *bow by night, grapple her, and gain surprise by sweeping her decks with musketry. But a certain Man, sympathetic to Lt. Simpson's jealousy, did not drop our Anchor when he ought and the plan was ruined. We managed to sail off still unrecognized by the sleepy English.*

On the 22nd, at night, we stood off Whitehaven in the Firth of Forth. Capt. Jones commanded one of two boats going ashore, and I was with him. Lts. Hill and Wallingsford in the other were ordered to set fire to a mass of ships in the north part of the Harbor. When we got ashore we left some men ready to fire other shipping close by. The rest of us then Rowed under the walls of the Fort.

Having no scaling ladders, we stood on each other's shoulders. I was first through a cannon embrasure. Pistol and cutlass in hand, I crouched a moment in the blackness. Then I saw a sentry lean-

ing against a wall, asleep. Other men entering other embrasures along the fortress wall waited as I did for the Signal.

It came. Just as the sentry stirred, I leapt on him and knocked him Senseless. In half an hour when daylight peeked over the World, we had scattered the Redcoats and spiked all their Cannon. Then with Capt. Jones and others I went along the top of the fort wall to its south side, which also commands the sea. In similar fashion we captured all the sentinels there, surprised the Garrison and held them captive, and ruined all their Cannon.

On our return to the shore we expected to see great fires from the shipping. But Lts. Hill and Wallingsford said just as they were ready to Ignite, their dark lanterns went out so they had no flame. 'Twas the same misfortune happened to us.

By now two or three thousand English folk had gathered. But as we showed Arms, they feared us and only stood at a distance. Capt. Jones seized my shoulder. "Noah, are we to lose out? I want those vessels yonder fired!" So I chose Tom Boyce and Abner Stilwell and we ran along the shore. By now some folk had got Guns and fired at us, but their aim was notably Poor. We three reached a cluster of schooners and went aboard a center one. While Tom and Abner upset a barrel of tar, I opened our reserve dark lantern. We lighted the tar. Flames spread so fast we scarce could flee them without being burned. We leapt to the dock and ran back to our Party, which now was holding at bay a great crowd, and there was much shooting.

Tom Boyce's hat swept off with a Bullet and one passed through my coat. But we reached our boats, manned, and lying in the Surf. "Hurry!" Capt. Jones called, for the Redcoats had got into action two Fort cannon somehow overlooked and were hurling balls at us.

We waded out, jumped in the boat, and were rowed away. Heedless of the firing our Capt. stood in the stern sheets, gazing at the flames that went ever higher, consuming rapidly several dozen enemy Vessels. So that was our adventure, save that our Capt. had hoped to burn 200 Vessels.

Next day we landed at St. Mary's Isle, and here in a great Mansion resides the Earl of Selkirk on whose estate Capt. Jones was born. Being slightly wounded in the leg, I was kept with Capt. Jones when we went ashore. He kept pacing the beach but sent Lt. Simpson and some men to the Mansion. Soon they returned bearing all the Silver Plate of the place, reporting that the Earl was absent. Capt. Jones was sore vexed at that. He had sought to capture the Earl so as later to exchange him for many American prisoners. At any rate, we burned a few Vessels, stood off hundreds of cowardly natives, and returned to our ship.

And that, Eileen, is all my news to now. But I shall have more, for we are again off Carrick Fergus and word is that H.M.S. Drake, *20 guns, is coming out to sea. There sounds the Call to Stations! I must be to duty, for I doubt not we shall now have a Great Battle.*

As Noah ran on deck he saw the British ship far to shoreward but moving. One of her small boats was rowing toward the *Ranger* which barely kept headway under scant sail. Captain Jones on the quarterdeck gave an order to Lieutenant Simpson. The Lieutenant beckoned to Noah and five others to take up stations at the rope ladder overside.

Presently a lieutenant from the *Drake,* followed by three seamen, clambered over the *Ranger's* rail. He brushed his gold-braided cuffs as he gazed contemptuously at Lieutenant Simpson, then up and down the *Ranger's* deck.

"What vessel is this? Where are you bound? Show me your commander and your papers!"

Lieutenant Simpson smiled a little, though the enemy's condescension made Noah grip his fists. "This is the United States man-o-war 'Ranger.' And you, sir, are our prisoners."

The Englishman's jaw slackened. He looked thunderstruck. "M-Man-o'-war? United S-States?"

Lieutenant Simpson's signal made Noah and his

"What Vessel Is This?" Demanded the Britisher

mates whip out pistols to cover the strangers. The Lieutenant, still smiling, extended his hand.

"Your sword, sir. Then I shall conduct you below. Like you Redcoats, we have a place always ready to contain captives."

Captain Jones watched while the astonished English were taken below. Meanwhile, observing that the *Drake* worked but slowly out of harbor, he caused the *Ranger* to beat back and forth, waiting. After nearly an hour of tension, the British vessel came within hail.

"Hullo!" someone called from her. "What ship is that?"

Captain Jones himself replied. "We are the Continental ship 'Ranger.' We have waited for you, and desire you to come out. There's scarce an hour before the sun sets, and I intend to have you captive before dark!"

Noah and all the other men on deck gave a cheer. Red Cherry at the helm put it hard over on order. Noah ran to his gun station forward. At his sharp command the rail port was hooked back and the Long Tom's muzzle run through. At the same time the Stars and Stripes rippled out at the forepeak.

"Mr. Simpson," Captain Jones said coolly, "when we cross her bow you may give her a broadside."

An instant later the *Ranger* shuddered at the roar of all her port cannon. Sweeping the *Drake's* main deck at only a hundred and twenty yards, the grapeshot was like a broom. It cleared almost every man from the deck. It split the Britisher's mainmast and riddled her after deckhouse.

The ships moved apart. With short, curt orders Captain Jones maneuvered, seeking another such opportunity. The guns were to fire lower next time, some at the waterline, others into the between-decks armament of the *Drake.*

But the Britisher too could maneuver. She also had fire power! Her broadside from off the port quarter sent wood splinters flying. A man at the gun next Noah's whipped around, spun crazily to amidships, and pitched to deck with blood streaming from his head where a shell fragment had taken him. And although Surgeon Walter and his aides rushed to his assistance, he was dead.

Below decks the *Ranger* took worse punishment—but gave it also below decks on the *Drake.* Each vessel sought to smash the heavy armament of the other, and it was between decks that the greatest number of guns were mounted. Cruising under full sail, each commander strove to provide himself the best opening. Now the *Drake* almost achieved a broadside attack . . .

"Hard a-starb'd!" Noah heard Red Cherry repeat an order as he spun the wheel.

The *Drake,* standing off but a quarter-mile, spat

red flame from her gun ports. Noah had but time to glimpse it when he flung down his upraised hand and Tom Boyce jerked the lanyard of the Long Tom. The weapon recoiled twelve feet back on the deck, halted by the eight-inch-thick hawsers. At that instant a solid shot whizzed close overhead with such speed that Noah thought his hair would be jerked from his scalp. Men spilled around him at the force of the suction and he staggered, but kept his feet.

A cry went up. Tom Boyce, clutching the gun-mount as he got erect, stared at the foe. "Noah! We took her main-tops'l!"

Indeed it was true. Canvas flopped dangling from the *Drake's* upper mast. Now the *Ranger* had warped about . . .

"*Fire!*" cried Lieutenant Simpson at the brief advantage.

Noah's gun, however, was being moved back to its exact position painted on the deck. But four guns below belched out—and again Tom Boyce shouted in triumph. Noah had no time to look, urging his crew to swifter swabbing, then loading.

"It's her mizzen!" someone shouted.

"Aim your best, Tom!" Noah, cool though the blood raced through him, put his ear close to his pointer's. "Let's carry off her mainmast. Take your time. Aim well!"

Their gun stood ready. Squinting, Tom made his sights. The *Ranger* heaved back at the impact of solid shot tearing low into her side. She wallowed, righted herself—heeled again on her beam-ends as the between-decks port battery thundered once more.

Tensely the forward gun crew waited. Suddenly Tom jerked the lanyard. Again the heavy cannon whipped back against its restraining ropes. When the smoke cleared the anxious gun crew peered at the foe.

They groaned. Their shot must have gone wild.

But the two ships, Noah realized suddenly, were closing.

"Hold your fire!"

The word passed along. "Hold your fire!"

Then: "Marines! Ready to board! Seamen! Grappling irons out for'ard!"

The company of marines aboard the *Ranger*, bold men and armed to the teeth, assembled in knots along her starboard side as she made a complete turn. The wind filled her topsails and she bore back. The *Drake,* seeking to elude, had luffed. But the American stole her wind in her own sails and the enemy lay wallowing.

Now she was growing larger as the *Ranger* bore close. Fascinated, Noah moved automatically at the order:

"Gun crews, main deck! Get small arms! Ready to board!"

As one man, Noah's crew dove for the stand of muskets, pistols, and cutlasses around the mainmast. Noah seized a pistol, thrust it in his belt, and snatched up a cutlass. He rushed for the forward starboard bow. There was no further use for the deck gun or any formation now. Every man was expected to join the marines and when the two vessels touched, to swarm aboard the enemy while sailors fixed their grappling irons and the two ships were clewed together.

The *Drake* seemed to be unmanageable, the way she came on without veering left or right. The *Ranger's* bow struck her just forward of amidships with a glancing blow that would have jarred everyone to his knees were he unready for the shock. Then the genius of Captain Jones went a step farther as Noah saw the glancing blow had swung the *Ranger* sideways. While the vessels jarred apart, a last point-blank blast came from three of her between-decks six-pounders.

The *Drake,* caught by grappling irons, heeled over on her side. When she rolled back to balance, the marines were leaping from their own rail to hers. Noah made the jump—landed on his feet—felt a pistol bullet spit hotly along his neck. A burly Jack Tar plunged at him with a cutlass . . .

The Marines Were Leaping Over Her Rail

"We have struck!"

Noah leaped aside from his foe's charge. The cry repeated over the *Drake's* main deck and was echoed from the *Ranger.*

"Cease firing! She has struck!"

The burly Jack Tar glared evilly as he lowered his cutlass. Noah held out his hand and the man surrendered the knife.

By now a great number of *Ranger* men were aboard the *Drake* and it was short work disarming the enemy and rounding them up in knots on her deck. As Noah added to his letter to Eileen the following day:

The battle lasted an hour and 4 minutes to capture H.M.S. Drake. *The ships were evenly matched, the* Drake *having 20 four-pounders to our 18 six-pounders. However, as Capt. Jones declared ere we ever left Nantes, our cannon are too short-barreled to be most effective. And the foe numbered many more men. But we gained the advantage in our first broadsides and managed to keep it.*

Lt. Wallingsford was killed and one seaman, and we suffered six men wounded, including Midshipman Powers who lost his arm. The enemy lost in killed and wounded 42 men. Their Capt. received a musket ball in the Head a moment before they cried for Quarter, and died soon after. Their highest Lt. died today and we have buried both gentlemen with honors due their valiant spirits.

We are bound back to France now. We are taking the Drake *to show Frenchmen that Americans can fight George the Third's men-o'-war and win!*

No one knows when we shall Voyage again but I hope soon. We learn that our Whitehaven raid frightened all England half out of her Wits. Vessel insurance rates have doubled. Folks are demanding their Fleet be called home for protection. Some stories have it that we number 12 sail, though of course we have but one. So 'tis plain, Eileen, that Capt. Jones's plan, which he first Broached in the Virginia House the night I hid from Mr. MacAuliffe in your trunk—that 'twas indeed a Sound Plan to throw Fear into our enemy by scourging his Coast.

That is all the news. I am in good health and trust you are also.

Noah Carr, midshipman,
U.S.S. Ranger,
At Sea, April 25, 1778.

CHAPTER FIFTEEN

BONHOMME RICHARD VS. SERAPIS

Doctor Benjamin Franklin was stouter than when Noah had last seen him, and he looked older. He was troubled with gout and though he let it interfere little with accomplishing his duties, he was often in pain. Too, responsibility had aged the good Doctor. For a long time he alone had represented the United States in France, striving to win her assistance in fighting England. Now he was one of three commissioners, of whom it was said that Mr. Silas Deane was co-operative but the vain and jealous Mr. Richard Henry Lee caused Doctor Franklin much trouble.

He was in his study in the mansion in Passy, near Paris. Quite bald, he made a round little figure sitting in his bathrobe, his gouty foot on a stool. Doctor Franklin studied Noah's indenture agreement a long time, peering at it over his half-lensed spectacles, then scrutinizing it through a magnifying glass.

"Well, now." He looked at Noah, seated near by. "Captain Jones told you to consult me about this?"

"Yes, sir. I feel strongly, sir, that my mother had property and that I was meant to be a gentleman, not a bound-boy. Since Mr. Angus MacAuliffe has been proved a spy, Captain Jones thinks as I do, that he might also have been capable of trickery toward me.

"Sir," Noah pleaded, " 'tis not much to go on, I'm aware. But it has always been in my heart that something's queer about my being indentured. I thought—well, I would greatly value your opinion what I should do, Dr. Franklin."

The kind old man studied him over his spectacles. "Can you add any information about your father?"

"I'm afraid, sir, I've told all I know. We lived on a sort of farm near Trinidad. My father died when I was but five. Mother sold the plantation. I had the impression she purchased another, but I was so young such matters did not mean much to me."

"Well, you can leave this indenture with me if you wish. I see it bears the witness signature of a Margaret O'Dowd and that 'twas written in Norfolk. I shall make inquiries to America." He looked across the table at Noah and smiled. "So you kept the penny I gave you that morning in Philadelphia?"

Noah showed it in his hand. "I shall always keep it, Doctor Franklin, as a remembrance of your kindness to a stranger."

"Come, come." But he was pleased. "Let it remind you, rather, to always be industrious. Well, Noah," he added, offering a packet of papers, "kindly hand these to Captain Jones with my compliments. You will be sailing soon and I look forward to more naval exploits as punishing to the enemy as was your last. God bless you, my boy," Doctor Franklin said, and shook hands.

It was Noah's last of several messenger errands between his commander and persons of importance in Paris, Passy, and the seat of French Government in Versailles. A few days later he was at sea on a cruise destined to make history.

It was not in the *Ranger* Captain Jones sailed this time, for the old ship had long been discarded. Nor was it in the *Indien,* which French gold had built for John Paul Jones in Holland. For the alert British had discovered the *Indien* and demanded sternly of Holland: "You are at peace with us, yet you build this vessel for the Americans to fight us. Why?" The frightened Dutch protested that the *Indien* was for France. To make their story seem true, France had taken the vessel into her navy.

That was the cause of great delay. Captain Jones, seeking another vessel, got promises aplenty but all were broken. Words of encouragement buoyed him up but were forgotten and brought discouragement. A whole summer, autumn, and spring passed with his crew idle, unpaid, and often starving while he negotiated, pleaded, threatened, and begged. He consumed his own fortune to pay his waiting sailors, until he no longer had funds. Congress failed to send money; the commissioners bickered among themselves; the French Government had consented to an alliance but still was slow in helping Captain Jones.

Many times Noah had seen Captain Jones pale and thin with anxiety. Many times he had been white with anger when his plans came to naught. Many times, yearning to be at sea and fighting, he had been plunged into despair of ever again casting off his lines. But always he rallied, pounded his fist on the table, and with new hope started new plans to challenge the ill-fortune that dogged him.

Now, at long last, with the Stars and Stripes flying proudly above her, the *Bonhomme Richard* was at sea.

She had been called the *Duras*, this former East Indiaman which France had presented to the United States. Captain Jones renamed her in honor of Poor Richard, the famous character in Doctor Franklin's writings, and put the name in French to honor France. She had been rebuilt at L'Orient under his supervision, fitted with 42 guns, and had a trial cruise escorting merchantmen along the coast. Experience showed she was a slow and cumbersome sailer, and her armament was cast off from the French Navy and poor and likely to explode. Nevertheless she was a fighting ship. Impatient of further delay, Captain Jones was setting out on another voyage to harass shipping along the coasts of England.

It was spring of 1779, and Noah found it hard to believe he had been a sailor four years. Though much had happened in that time: he had sailed the length of the North American coast, crossed the Atlantic, sailed around Ireland and England, and along the coast of France. In dozens of fierce sea battles he had seen John Paul Jones emerge victor—a hard, dauntless, resourceful fighter and a superb navigator. Against all save unarmed merchant ships he always contended with a greener crew, a poorer vessel, and inferior armament. Yet his genius had won him world renown as a commander.

Noah—he was Midshipman Carr now—stood near Red Cherry at the helm as the ponderous *Bonhomme Richard* plowed through the North Sea. In five weeks they had made almost a complete circle of the British Isles and had captured a score of enemy ships. Most of these had been sunk, a few sent back manned by prize crews. The original squadron of six under Captain Jones's command had been reduced to four by jealousy among the captains due to inexact orders from the American commissioners. Only the *Pallas*, *Vengeance*, and *Alliance* now remained with the *Bonhomme Richard*. The first two were but small vessels. The third was commanded by Captain Pierre Landais, a Frenchman who professed a desire to fight for the United States but who hated Captain Jones and repeatedly ignored his orders.

"Him no good," Red Cherry declared. "He never do what Captain say. Him shoot us sometime," he prophesied darkly.

At a cry from the crow's-nest Noah gazed across the starboard bow. "Look!" he ejaculated. "Ship after ship! Still they keep coming!"

They stood watching the procession of white sails appearing around the tip of Flamborough Head, which projected far out to sea. The vessels were like a covey of quail, scudding peacefully along under light breeze. Noah saw Captain Jones at the rail watching them through his glass.

"Baltic Fleet," Red Cherry breathed. "We hunt long time. Now we find, eh? How many you count?"

"Two men-o'-war there in the lead," Captain Jones remarked to Lieutenant Fanning at his elbow. "Signal the *Pallas*, *Vengeance*, and *Alliance* to fall into line of battle. We'll not sound our general alarm yet, Mr. Fanning, as we won't get close to our friends for some time."

Noah whistled. "I count forty-one merchantmen and the two men-o'-war!"

"Yes. Now merchantmen turn and run home." He chuckled. "But men-o'-war not afraid. They come."

He glanced aft. "See? *Pallas* and *Vengeance* obey Captain Jones. But *Alliance* go off by herself."

Angrily Noah saw he was right. Why did Captain Landais ignore the order to fall into battle line? For indeed he had changed course and was leaving the scene. Captain Jones's face was taut with contempt.

"Coward!" he snapped.

A great battle was brewing: one could feel it in the air. Word went around that the British fighting ships were the *Serapis* and the *Countess of Scarborough.* It was one o'clock in the afternoon when the two fleets sighted each other from many miles' distance, but it might be several hours before firing commenced.

The afternoon wore on. With her two small fighting ships behind her, the *Bonhomme Richard* sailed to engage the leading foe. Meanwhile, the convoyed merchantmen had run back behind Flamborough Head for the port of Scarborough. H.M.S. *Serapis* brought to, keeping out of danger while she awaited the support of the *Countess of Scarborough* when the merchant vessels had been escorted to safety from the Yankee raiders whom all England feared.

At five o'clock the *Countess* reappeared and made to join the *Serapis.* Signaling the *Pallas* and *Vengeance,* Captain Jones directed them at the *Countess.* Meanwhile he maneuvered to get the shore on his starboard and the *Serapis* to port. It was seven o'clock before the battle-ready *Bonhomme Richard* came within hail of the enemy.

"She's fifty guns," Tom Boyce worried, "and a better ship all around than this old tub. She's brand-new and we're twelve years old. And I doubt not her crew's well trained. And we've five hundred prisoners below to make trouble for us!"

"We've been hunting Redcoats and there they are," Noah rejoined.

"Aye, but this'll be a battle like none we've ever had. I'm glad we've got the marines, even if they do talk a jaw-jaw nobody can understand." Tom indicated Colonel Chamillard and his companies of French marines clustered on the old-fashioned poop and scattered in groups about the main deck.

Slowly twilight set in. All along the distant shore of Flamborough Head crowds of civilians waited to watch the battle. Aboard the *Bonhomme Richard* every crewman was at his station, every gun-pointer ready. Slow matches were lighted, powder monkeys had piled bags of powder and shot and solid iron balls.

Silence gripped the *Bonhomme Richard*. The vessels were closing in, beam to beam. There came a hail.

"What–ship–is–that?"

Wanting another minute to drop his vessel a little

farther astern of the other, Captain Jones replied, "I can't hear what you say."

"Answer immediately or I shall be under the necessity of firing on you!"

Captain Jones raised his arm and let it fall.

"Fire!" cried Lieutenant Fanning.

"*Fire!*" echoed throughout the ship.

She reeled back as tongues of flame slashed from her port guns below and on deck, and the few mounted on the poop. Noah, in charge of a Long Tom on the main deck, saw vivid flashes of flame leap at the same instant from the *Serapis*. Then he felt the *Richard* heel farther onto her beam than usual as the weight of metal from the enemy pounded into her sides.

There came an explosion below. The deck lifted and burst. Two of the *Richard's* guns had blown to bits when fired. Dazed, Noah was flung so hard against the butt of the mainmast that he lay a moment, fighting for breath.

He got to his feet. He seemed unhurt, only bruised. His Long Tom had been blown overboard.

Astounded, he saw a gaping hole in the side and main deck of the *Bonhomme Richard*. Cries of wounded men came to his ears. Then another broadside spat in red tongues from the *Serapis*, and next instant flames licked upward from the rent side of the *Richard*.

She was afire!

"—get the men out!" came the ringing tones of Captain Jones. Noah saw him peering down into the huge hole in his vessel that was a blazing inferno. "Close those ports, Mr. Hall!"

He whirled and barked orders to Red Cherry at the helm. The *Serapis* fired again, from a battery between decks hitherto unsuspected. Again the *Richard* reeled at the blow; but gradually, under Red Cherry's cool maneuvering, she drew away.

But the fight, Noah knew with misgivings, had started badly.

"Some of our braces are gone. She scarcely answers the helm," a man growled.

"We're done for! That Britisher's twice our size. Why'd the fool have to go at her like we were a hundred guns?"

Noah turned on the speaker. "Leave command to the Captain. Get to your work!"

The man blinked. Before he could answer, Noah grabbed his shoulder and gave him a shove. "Get to that next gun!"

He glanced about for others of his gun crew. Hardman, the pointer, was calmly taking the place of a man killed. Simms, Foley, and Eustace were nowhere to be seen. Perhaps they had lost their lives in the below-decks explosion.

Well, Noah no longer had a gun to command.

His eyes fell on a powder monkey groaning on the deck. Stepping to him, Noah gently lifted and carried him aft to where Doctor Walter, the surgeon, was already trying to do the work of four men.

A minute later Noah was himself a powder boy. He stood at the opening to the main powder hatch, taking heavy bags handed up to him and running with them to the deck guns. Next it was shells, heavy and slippery in his hands.

The wind now was light. The vessels jockeyed for position. The *Richard*, always a heavy sailer, responded slowly to her canvas. The *Serapis* seemed to have discovered this, for she kept off the stern quarter, raking the American vessel with repeated murderous broadsides.

And they were doing terrible damage! Noah's heart quaked as he glanced at the wreckage-strewn deck. The main topgallants had been shot away, and, spilling down, they created extra confusion. Men with axes hacked at the splintered spars. Others hauled the sail fragments to the side and flung them overboard.

All up and down the deck lay the wreckage of guns, men wounded and bleeding, and smashed equipment. The fire between decks still raged, though Noah thought it seemed not to have spread much. The *Bonhomme Richard* listed to port like a wounded animal limping. She was settling, too, he

The Richard *Listed Like a Wounded Animal*

thought—taking water.

"Mr. Carr!"

He jumped. He ran across the littered deck and up the short ladder to the poop. "Aye, aye, sir!"

Captain Jones looked as calm and unruffled as he had after breakfast this morning. "Go below. Tell Lieutenant Hall to get more prisoners working the pumps. Tell them if they don't want to drown like rats, they'd best keep us afloat."

"Aye, aye, sir."

"And report to me how badly we're off down there."

Noah ran down the ladder and to the after companionway. The jar of a *Serapis* broadside hurled him sprawling. He picked himself up, ignoring his new bruises as he went down the companionway.

At sight of the gun-deck wreckage he paused, his heart skipping a beat. It was hot down there from the flames crackling close by. Men lay groaning, begging for water. The ancient French cannon that had exploded lay about in hot chunks of metal.

With grim-set jaw Noah continued on his errand. Now he could hear the pumps wheezing, hear sea water sloshing. The *Richard* was settling. . . At last, pulling open a bulkhead door, he found Lieutenant Hall, sword in one hand and pistol in the other and backed by four riflemen. They faced crowded hundreds of nervous captives taken from merchant ships and men-o'-war during the last five weeks.

Noah gave his message. In the eerie light of lanterns, Hall, eying the prisoners massed and sullen, repeated it. "Now will ye pump?" he barked. "Or drown?"

There was no response. Growling started in the humanity-packed hold like distant thunder. It came louder and the five hundred men surged slightly forward. Noah's heart stopped. Should they dare to attack there was no doubt they could overpower their handful of captors.

The muffled thunder of *Serapis* guns was swiftly followed by new reeling of the doomed *Bonhomme Richard*. Intermittently her own guns blasted, and she heeled over again. Balancing themselves to the rolling, the prisoners listened, scowling and on the verge of defiant rebellion.

"I'll count to five. When I've finished," Lieutenant Hall threatened, "ye'd better be working those pumps. Else I'll kill the front five men, then the next."

He started to count. At "three" no one had stirred. At "four" he raised his pistol and the riflemen took aim. Noah stood frozen with anxiety. For if the captives rebelled, the *Richard's* battle was lost here in her dark hold: the vessel could not continue.

At "five" there was split-second hesitation. Then as one man the prisoners turned and scattered to the abandoned pumps.

Lieutenant Hall's hand trembled as he lowered his pistol. His face was yellow in the feeble lantern light. "My compliments to Captain Jones, and tell him that if God is merciful we can float another hour."

Hastily Noah made his way back. Twice he was flung from ladders at terrific jars, as if the two vessels had collided. At last he climbed out of the companionway to a scene of confusion that made him halt, scarcely crediting his eyes.

"Our own *Alliance* gave us two broadsides!" Tom Boyce raged almost tearfully as he ran past. "Blast that Captain Landais! The traitor!"

He was gone. Noah glimpsed the *Alliance* pulling away. But evidently her treachery had not diverted Captain Jones's intention to keep battling.

The *Bonhomme Richard* now managed to turn close across the bow of the *Serapis*. The British vessel's bowsprit came plunging across the American's afterdeck. With the gentle swelling of the sea it splintered off with a great crash, and the vessels crunched their rails at quarter-length.

The fluke of the *Serapis's* anchor had caught forward. The ratlines and shrouds of the two vessels were intertangled.

After the first punishing broadsides had all but wrecked his ship this had been Captain Jones's great hope, to close with the *Serapis*. He had men with grappling irons securing the two vessels, though the *Serapis* sought to pull away. From the *Richard's* tops came a withering fire of muskets at those on the other deck. Noah saw Lieutenant Dale and a party of marines dash to the *Richard's* side, scatter, and begin to pick off with their muskets those manning the foe's deck guns. Captain Jones himself was helping to turn around a three-pounder so as to use it on the enemy's deck; and two others had already been reversed and were firing.

Noah started for his commander. At that instant Henson, the *Richard's* carpenter, ran up behind and pushed him out of his way. As Noah reeled he saw Jennings, the master-at-arms, and a gunner pelting up from below after Henson.

"They're shooting into our pumps! Captain Jones and Lieutenant Dale are killed!" Henson cried as if half-crazed. He ran as close to the rail as he could go and cupped both hands beside his mouth.

"Quarter!" he pleaded of the British. *"Give us quarter!"*

Thunderstruck, Noah watched and heard this plea for mercy. The man wanted to surrender!

He saw Captain Jones whip around at the words. As Noah darted to help him, Captain Jones jerked a pistol from his belt. He aimed it at Henson and pulled the trigger. It failed to explode. In fury, he whipped his arm back and hurled the weapon at the carpenter. It took Henson fair on the side of the head. He went reeling, stumbled, and sprawled on his side.

Noah grabbed Jennings's arm. He spun him around. "We're still fighting, man! To your station!"

Jennings, glancing dazedly from Henson at his feet to Noah, suddenly recovered himself. Noah let him go, and pistol in hand, sought to reach Captain Jones. Then came a hail from the *Serapis.*

"Ahoy, *Bonhomme Richard!* Have you struck?"

It was like the clap of doom. Silence fell. The men on the main deck of each ship froze like statues.

John Paul Jones rushed to the rail. He cupped both hands to his mouth. "*No!*" he bellowed in fury. "*I have just begun to fight!*"

Again, silence. Then cheers rang from the *Richard's* deck. Muskets resumed crackling. Two of the three-pounders blasted at once and their canister cleared a bloody lane across the deck of the *Serapis.*

Noah plucked his commander's sleeve. "Sir, Lieutenant Hall says he can keep us afloat another hour. And sir," he rushed on, offering his pistol, butt-first, "I borrowed one of these four years ago and wish now to return it."

"Eh?" Captain Jones's faded blue eyes went to the weapon, then to Noah's face. He took the pistol like a man striving to remember.

"You handed me a pistol four years ago when I badly needed it. Later, you asked for its return. I return it now, Captain Jones. But this is better than the one you gave me," he added. "It's loaded."

Remembrance came over John Paul Jones's face. His eyes gleamed. With his left hand he gave Noah a clap on the shoulder that was almost a shove.

"Well said! Now," he cried, "we want boarders! Come on! Let's finish 'em off!"

CHAPTER SIXTEEN

AFTER THE BATTLE

But it was not quite time for boarders, as the doughty British proved by annihilating with muskets and pistols the first group that leaped from rail to rail.

Repulsed, Captain Jones ordered Lieutenant Dale and a handful of sharpshooting marines up into the yards where some already perched, high above the deck, trying to pick off Jack Tars on the *Serapis*. Far out on the tip of a yardarm so that he looked down on the enemy's deck, Tom Boyce now straddled the spar while coolly he took grenades, one by one, from a bucket slung over his arm. Carefully he tossed them, trying to hit the ladder to the foe's main powder magazine. Meanwhile, on the *Richard's* deck, the three nine-pounders sprayed canister and grape that swept like brooms of death from rail to rail of the enemy's beam.

Noah was helping to man one of these cannon. As fast as canister could be loaded into the glowing-hot gun, he jerked the lanyard. The swabber, springing to his work, suddenly threw up his hands and fell. Noah grabbed his plunger, at the same time barking orders to the others of his little band.

Above the rattle of musketry and in a lull between the throaty pound of heavy guns on both ships came the cry, "The *Alliance!*"

" 'Twas a mistake she riddled us before. This'll save us!" Bos'n Green shouted.

It put new heart into every *Bonhomme Richard* man who heard. Noah had time for a glance forward and felt momentary surprise at the nearness of Captain Landais's vessel. She loomed like some ghostly specter close off the port bow; and the thought flashed through his mind that one broadside end-to-end of the *Serapis* as she lay now might thoroughly clean her deck for boarding.

Nor could there be any mistake in identity this time, for following Captain Landais's last blunder, the *Richard* had hoisted signal lanterns to her mastheads in a secret American code. So four-score others waited tensely like Noah for this nick-of-time aid. But the fire slashing from the whole starboard row of the *Alliance's* guns spat not at the *Serapis*—but again at the *Bonhomme Richard!*

She seemed to lift back on her stern at the slam of the metal. Fresh cries of pain sprang from wounded below and on deck, and a groan wrung from those unhurt proved their hate for this perfidy.

Why had Captain Landais again deliberately fired on the *Richard?* The man was stark mad!

"It's the third time!" moaned a fellow gunner.

"The fool! The traitor!" He fell speechless with rage.

"Quick, men! Clear her decks! Boarding party ready!"

That was Captain Jones's voice. If he too felt unspeakable rage at the rascally Captain Landais he did not waste precious moments voicing it. He had the British to deal with first, and kept darting here, there, barking an order, giving encouragement. Cool and self-possessed as if the *Bonhomme Richard* safely sailed a placid sea, the only discernible change in him was the rabbit-swiftness of his movements and talk.

Yet he had lost the battle long since, would he but acknowledge it. For his vessel bore a great hole in her main deck, wide enough to drive a coach-and-six through. The great gap showed the litter of cannon, timbers, and wounded and dying men on the deck below. The *Serapis,* clewed tightly now to the *Richard,* kept firing her heavy between-decks battery, the gun muzzles actually poking into the *Richard's* side. Again and again they thundered, tearing out the *Richard's* vitals with such force that some iron missiles went ripping full across her and through her far walls and into the sea beyond.

Both ships were afire. The *Serapis's* yards showed sails blazing like great torches against the peaceful moonlit sky, and there were smaller fires scattered the length of her hull. The *Richard's* plight was still worse than that of her enemy. The initial blaze had been controlled for awhile, but now crackled more greedily than ever on the oakum-soaked rotten timbers of her hull. Noah glimpsed Bos'n Green rushing to Captain Jones with the report.

"Nine fires, sir. We can't control 'em. We haven't the men!"

"Keep at it, Bos'n. Do the best you can. We're going to need this vessel awhile longer." He turned away to some challenge more urgent. As he did so, embers spilled on his shoulder from the burning mainmast; but he brushed them off as if scarcely noting.

Too, the *Richard* was sinking. Noah could feel her settle convulsively now and again, like some monster digging itself into earth. She listed drunkenly toward the *Serapis,* whose resisting mass kept her from tipping more.

Thus the hopeless battle raged. On deck, marines and sailors worked every available weapon. High above, often obscured by smoke, sharpshooters clung and picked off enemies on the *Serapis.* Out on his yardarm Tom Boyce coolly prepared to toss his last grenade. Below, on the gun-deck of the wrecked and sinking *Richard* was a great litter of dead and wounded men, broken cannon, and splintered and burning timbers. From time to time, with the heavy blast of the *Serapis's* broadside, the whole vessel seemed to half-lift out of the water at the pound of hot metal tearing through her.

"Captain Jones! The prisoners've escaped!"

That cry sent a cold lance through Noah. But as if it was merely one more problem to meet, Captain Jones darted to the aft companionway. The pistol in his fist leveled at the several captives in the front rank of those pelting up from the hold. Five hundred there were in all, and for an instant the five hundred were held at bay by one flashing-eyed bantam of a man.

"We're sinking! We'll capsize—" one of them began.

"Get below! It's the *Serapis* that's sinking, you fools!" Captain Jones cried. "Keep us afloat or we're all going down!"

Noah saw them hesitate. The audacious bluff hung like a sword suspended by a single silken thread. Then the magic of the man's personality won out. Believing him, the officers and crews of vessels captured on the *Richard's* cruise turned and crowded back below to again man the pumps.

Noah stood astounded. Had Captain Jones failed to persuade them, they were numerous enough, even though not armed, to have seized the *Richard* in a matter of minutes. They could have gained an historic victory for England. Instead, one man's commanding personality had snatched victory from them.

The battle kept on. The roar of guns large and small, the mounting, brightening flames from the two vessels burning in the night as they hugged in a death embrace, reddened the sea. And the enemy shore flung back reverberating gun-thunder like the mocking, evil laughter of doom.

A heavy explosion aboard the *Serapis* was followed by a ragged cheer from the Americans. Word spread that Tom Boyce's last grenade had gone down the hatchway at which he had long aimed. It exploded among cartridges laid out by powder monkeys. One cartridge set off the next, and the bursts rattled the entire way aft through crews manning the main battery. With a last tremendous roar the powder magazine blew up, killing twenty men in an instant.

This was the turning-point for which Captain Jones had waited. "*Now!*" he bellowed. "Lieutenant Dale, you may board her!"

Because of the grape, canister, and musket fire the main deck of the *Serapis* held few British to resist. Over the rail swarmed the Americans, Noah among them. Leaping over wounded and dead foemen, he rushed with Lieutenant Dale for the quarter-deck. As they ran up the short ladder Noah saw a British tar lowering the shot-riddled banner of England. Tears were streaming down his leathery face and he stared numbly at Noah as if not seeing him.

A tall, thin, elderly man with the gold braid of captain on his sleeves and shoulders stood on the lee side of the quarter-deck. Lieutenant Dale strode to him, Noah at his elbow.

"Sir," barked Lieutenant Dale, "I take it you have struck?"

He sighed heavily. "Yes. I have struck. I am Captain Pearson."

"My orders, sir, are to send you aboard the ship alongside."

They were interrupted by the first lieutenant of the *Serapis* striding up. "Captain Pearson, have the dogs struck to us at last?"

Captain Pearson was silent. Lieutenant Dale's smile was cold and grim.

"Lieutenant, it is the contrary. The *Serapis* has struck."

When the other had recovered somewhat from his astonishment, Dale added, "I have orders to escort both of you gentlemen to my commander."

He signed to Noah to accompany him. They followed the two discouraged officers aboard the *Richard*, where Lieutenant Dale introduced them to Captain Jones.

Captain Pearson drew his sword and offered it by its handle. "It is painful to me," he said angrily, "that I must resign this to a man who has fought with a halter around his neck."

Noah saw Captain Jones flinch. The insult arose from malicious English gossip that he was a traitor and a pirate. But as always he kept his temper.

"Sir, you have fought like a hero. I make no doubt your sovereign will reward you in a most ample manner."

As if shamed by this courtesy, Captain Pearson scowled. He said in a more civil tone, "What countrymen make up most of your crew?"

"Americans. All of them," Captain Jones replied proudly.

Captain Pearson nodded. "Then it has been diamond cutting diamond, for we are all of the same stock."

Firing had ceased; the battle was over. Wounded were given the first attention, with the surgeons of both vessels working at top speed on all brought to them, whether English or American. Half an hour later the lashings which held the vessels together were cut. The mainmast of the *Serapis*, broken and supported only by interlocking yards, pitched overboard with a tremendous splash, carrying the *Richard's* mizzenmast with it.

All hands then were pressed to fighting fire and water. The *Richard* was in imminent danger from both, and the *Serapis* had a dozen fires scattered from end to end. But Captain Jones's vessel was in much the worse plight. Her pumps were manned by a double force, yet the water kept inching higher. All that night and through the next morning fires were fought and pumps kept at top speed. Lest the powder magazine get ablaze, all its contents were dumped overboard. At noon the following day Captain Jones became convinced that the *Bonhomme Richard* could not be saved.

"If a breeze springs up, she'll fill," he decided. "We'll abandon ship, Mr. Fanning."

The wounded were transferred to the *Serapis* and to the *Pallas,* which was now standing by. She had captured the British *Countess of Scarborough* after an hour's hard fighting. Another American vessel, the *Vengeance,* had taken no part in any fight, merely stood off and watched. As to the *Alliance,* she had sped away under full sail. It was plain that her cowardly Captain Landais had striven his best to sink the *Bonhomme Richard.* That accomplished, he had expected easily with his fresh crew to capture the badly hurt *Serapis* and to claim her as totally his own victory.

Noah Carr followed the servant into the book-lined study in the mansion at Passy. Doctor Franklin sat as he had seen him last, with his gouty foot on a cushion, his half-lensed spectacles on his nose as he

"You Have Served Your Country Well."

studied some papers. The servant withdrew and Noah, hat in hand, waited.

"Young man," said Doctor Franklin without glancing up, "do you still carry that penny I gave you?"

Noah laughed. "I'll always have it, sir, if you ask me twenty years hence."

Smiling, Doctor Franklin put down the papers and waved him to a chair. "I've heard all about that fierce battle," he said. "I have studied Captain Jones's report and the account of Captain Pearson. My boy, do you realize you took part in one of the greatest naval engagements ever fought?"

Noah swallowed. "Yes, sir. No one can ever say enough for the courage and resource of Captain Jones."

"You are right. He will go into the pages of history. In time I think he'll be considered the father of the American Navy. And you," he added, "fought as well as any. I've inquired into that also. I congratulate you, Noah. You have served your country well."

Embarrassed, Noah stared at the floor as he thanked the good Doctor.

"But I sent for you to deliver news. Oh!" he remembered, and shuffled among his papers for a letter. "This arrived for you." Doctor Franklin sniffed it before he handed it over. "Men don't use perfume like that, nor is it addressed in a male hand," he said with twinkling eyes.

With a glance Noah saw that it was from Eileen MacAuliffe.

"Before you read it, let me tell you what I've learned. In that letter, I doubt not, will be the same news that Mr. Angus MacAuliffe is dead."

Noah stared. "Dead! Mr. MacAuliffe?"

"Yes. Hanged as a spy in Portsmouth, together with Sergeant Beatty, whom you also captured."

"Yes, sir." He still was astonished. "We captured them just before the 'Ranger' sailed."

"Well, the note you left behind and your affidavit made in Captain Jones's cabin and witnessed by him, started a thorough investigation. Mr. MacAuliffe, we know now, was cashiered from the English Navy many years ago for cowardice. That same cowardice unnerved him and made him confess at the court-martial that your accusation of spying was correct."

Noah sat trying to absorb the fact that the man to whom he was indentured, was dead.

"Then I am free, Doctor Franklin?" he asked uncertainly.

"You're not only free, but a landed gentleman."

Noah frowned. "A—landed—gentleman?"

"Just so. I'll try to give an organized story. When you told me about yourself months ago, I promised to inquire in your behalf. And I did so. The combination of Mr. MacAuliffe's confession and my investigation by correspondence helps me put all the pieces together.

"Your father," he said, "was a well-to-do planter in Trinidad, West Indies. Back in England he had fallen in love with a young lady whose parents would not consent to their marriage. So they fled on the handiest vessel. A few years later this James Noah Carr, a good businessman, no doubt, owned a plantation near Trinidad. However, he died when you were but five years old.

"Overseer of his plantation was one Angus MacAuliffe. Evidently your father trusted this rascal, hence your mother, left a widow, did the same. After a few years she desired to leave Trinidad where her health was suffering. She sold her plantation, gave MacAuliffe half the proceeds, and sent him on to Virginia to buy her a new home."

"You mean—" Noah began excitedly.

"Hold on, please. MacAuliffe bought a plantation, worked it, asked for more money, received it, and invested in more land. Your mother kept wanting to come there. But MacAuliffe, who had purchased the place in his own name—the scoundrel!—kept persuading her that it was not ready and suitable. It wasn't yet 'civilized,' he wrote her.

"Becoming suspicious, your mother brought you to Norfolk. MacAuliffe met her there several times, always persuading her not to come on yet to Virginia—I mean, to the plantation. He feared exposure, of course. At last, on one of these visits, he found her with typhoid fever. Seeing that she might die, he suggested she make out a will. And here," Doctor Franklin said, "is where your indenture came in."

Noah sat on the edge of his chair. "Yes, sir?"

"We have MacAuliffe's confession, plus the testimony of a Negro, Zel, and that of a Mrs. O'Dowd, in whose Norfolk home your mother died. It seems MacAuliffe wrote out your mother's will and had her sign it. The same night he wrote out an indenture agreement, and after much practice copying your mother's signature on the will, signed her name to it.

"But MacAuliffe bungled his first forgery and discarded it," Doctor Franklin explained. "Mrs. O'-Dowd fortunately has preserved that copy. She watched MacAuliffe rewrite the indenture and carefully copy your mother's signature a second time. He discovered Mrs. O'Dowd observing him, and she demanded pay for her silence. The rascal was compelled to pay her regularly for keeping his secret, and she always kept the bungled indenture copy as a sort of threat over him. However, the woman has now been frightened into a full confession. So that, Noah, is how you became a bound-boy."

"Oh, sir!" Noah felt dazed. "I can scarce believe it!"

"By the wav," Doctor Franklin added, "the will named MacAuliffe as your guardian until you were twenty-one. How old are you now?"

"I shall be twenty-one, sir, in two months."

"Ah! Then I feel sure the entire matter will easily be adjusted to your satisfaction." He studied Noah. "Do you quite understand all this?"

"I—think so, sir. Does it mean the plantation is mine?"

"Indeed yes. 'Twas bought with your mother's funds, which she got from your father. The place is absolutely yours. Imagine! That rascal MacAuliffe not only deceived and robbed your mother, but actually got you indentured to help him work property rightfully yours!

"I'll give you a letter to an excellent lawyer in Virginia," he went on. "He knows your case—in fact, he wrung the confession from Mrs. O'Dowd. He'll help you regain all that is yours. Maybe you've heard of him—Mr. Patrick Henry?"

Noah grinned. "Indeed, I do know him. And I've full trust in Mr. Henry."

"Then your future is assured. You no longer are a bound-boy but a landowner. By the way, are you remaining in the Navy?"

"No, sir. General Washington's victories, I'm told,

virtually mean the end of the war. And in a battle along our coast I received a shell fragment in my arm which sometimes gives me trouble. So I've decided to return to the United States along with other members of Captain Jones's crew."

"Hmm. Well, read your letter now while I continue with my work."

As Doctor Franklin busied himself, Noah opened the letter from Eileen:

Oh, Noah, isn't it wonderful news? Papa just told me that Mr. Jos. Hewes told him how he assisted Doctor Franklin in investigating for your sake. You are no bound-boy at all, but a landowner! I do apologize, Noah, for mine own uncle being such a rascal as Angus MacAuliffe was, but it explains why I never liked him, nor did you. Papa too is shocked at his own brother acting so, and sends you his apology.

He read on a little farther where, after recounting the parties she had attended lately and the bandages she had made for soldier wounded, Eileen ended:

Noah, I wonder will I ever see your plantation again? Without my uncle, and with you owning it, I do think 'twill become a splendid place. Mammy Fanny and Zel will be so happy having you as their master! And may be some day I'll be in Virginia and can come and visit you.

"Well?"

Noah looked up to find Doctor Franklin's eyes on

him. "What does the little lady say? Is it friendly?"

"Oh, yes, sir. She wants to come visit me when I'm back on the plantation. And faith, I'll see she gets there, never fear!" Then as the Doctor laughed, Noah felt himself redden at thus impulsively confiding how much he liked Eileen MacAuliffe.

The door opened and Captain John Paul Jones entered. Noah sprang to his feet and came rigidly to attention. But Captain Jones, with a smile, gestured for him to be at ease.

"So you're homebound?" he said. "Going back to your own lands, so I hear."

"Yes, sir. But I shall never forget the privilege of serving under you, Captain Jones. And I should esteem it an honor if some time you'll visit me in Virginia."

"I should be pleased to do so, and perhaps some day I can." He glanced at Eileen's letter which Noah held. "I dare say Miss MacAuliffe is as charming and pert as ever? And that she'll give you a warm welcome, Noah." He laughed, poking Noah's ribs. "You didn't suppose I'd recall her name all these years, eh? But I wish you success in that matter, and much happiness."

Noah's deep crimson blush conveyed his thanks for this. After a moment he stepped closer to Doctor Franklin's desk.

"Sir, I have no words to express my thanks for

all you've done for me. I can only hope you will call on me sometime to pay some of the great debt I owe you."

"Come, come. 'Twas nothing," the old man assured. Then his eyes twinkled over his half-lensed spectacles as he grasped Noah's hand. "Mind never to lose that penny. Nor forget what it means!"

"I never shall, Doctor Franklin. And thank you from the bottom of my heart."

He turned to Captain Jones, who also shook hands.

"Sir, I owe you very much also. It began that day when I was plowing Mr. MacAuliffe's—I mean *my* field. Then when you handed me the pistol that night in the Virginia House so I could escape him. Later, you told me to learn to become a seaman—"

"And you became a good one. You could have a fine career in our new Navy. But," he smiled, "I guess you're a landlubber at heart?"

"Yes, sir, save when our country faces enemies. But I do thank you for all you've done and for your friendship, Captain Jones."

John Paul Jones gripped his hand a long moment. Releasing it, he put his arm around Noah's shoulders and walked with him to the door.

"You are young, Noah. Continue your part in building our new country. Serve our flag as a citizen as well as you've served it at sea. And if there are enough like you, 'twill build the greatest nation of free men this world has ever known. God bless you!"

Noah gazed a last time into the brave, faded blue eyes of the man who, though reason told him all was lost, had cried: *"I have just begun to fight!"* —and who had then battled on to victory.

The door closed. It closed on the good Doctor Benjamin Franklin and on the courageous John Paul Jones. It closed on the life of a bound-boy who became a sailor to help his country win its freedom.

Noah Carr was homebound to a new and great nation.

WHITMAN
AUTHORIZED EDITIONS

JANE WITHERS and the Swamp Wizard

JANE WITHERS and the Phantom Violin

JANE WITHERS and the Hidden Room

BONITA GRANVILLE and the Mystery of Star Island

ANN RUTHERFORD and the Key to Nightmare Hall

POLLY THE POWERS MODEL: The Puzzle of the Haunted Camera

JOYCE AND THE SECRET SQUADRON: A Captain Midnight Adventure

NINA AND SKEEZIX (of "Gasoline Alley"): The Problem of the Lost Ring

GINGER ROGERS and the Riddle of the Scarlet Cloak

SMILIN' JACK and the Daredevil Girl Pilot

APRIL KANE AND THE DRAGON LADY: A "Terry and the Pirates" Adventure

SHIRLEY TEMPLE and the Spirit of Dragonwood

ROY ROGERS and the Gopher Creek Gunman

GENE AUTRY and the Thief River Outlaws

RED RYDER and the Mystery of the Whispering Walls

RED RYDER and the Secret of Wolf Canyon